MAY - 3 2012

W9-BUV-940

COMPLEX 90
A MIKE HAMMER NOVEL

COMPLEX 90

A MIKE HAMMER NOVEL

MICKEY SPILLANE
and
MAX ALLAN COLLINS

TITANBOOKS

Complex 90: A Mike Hammer Novel
Print edition ISBN: 9780857684660
E-book edition ISBN: 9780857689535

Published by Titan Books
A division of Titan Publishing Group Ltd
144 Southwark St, London SE1 0UP

First edition: May 2013

1 3 5 7 9 10 8 6 4 2

A CIP catalogue record for this title is available from the British Library.

Printed and bound in the United States.

Did you enjoy this book? We love to hear from our readers. Please email us at readerfeedback@titanemail.com or write to us at Reader Feedback at the above address.

To receive advance information, news, competitions, and exclusive Titan offers online, please sign up for the Titan newsletter on our website: www.titanbooks.com

FOR CARL AMARI –

who brought Mike Hammer to life in his audio productions

CO-AUTHOR'S NOTE

In 1982, on a visit to Mickey Spillane's South Carolina home, I was handed by my host two substantial Mike Hammer manuscripts, *The Big Bang* and *Complex 90*.

I was flabbergasted—there hadn't been a Hammer published since 1970! And I recognized the title *Complex 90*, which had been announced for publication in the 1960s but never appeared. I read late into the night, and the next morning at breakfast offered up enthusiastic reviews.

"Maybe we can do something with 'em some day," he said casually. On a later visit, in 1989, he sent the partial manuscripts back to Iowa with me "for safekeeping."

Mickey's words proved prophetic: just weeks later, Hurricane Hugo destroyed his home. Both *Complex 90* and *The Big Bang* (2010) might well have been lost.

The setting is 1964 and the novel is, in part, a sequel to the Mike Hammer comeback novel of 1961, *The Girl Hunters*, the film version of which starred Mickey Spillane himself. While reading this novel, you are encouraged to picture Mike Hammer in just that way.

I am indebted to John Gunther's *Inside Russia Today* (1958) for Russian color.

M.A.C.

CHAPTER ONE

The older of the pair of armed M.P.s flanking me opened the door and stood there, waiting. Did they think I was going to try something, here in the heart of the Pentagon? Or was that the bowels?

I grinned at them, as if to say, *Not a chance, fellas.* Not without my .45, anyway.

Behind me, the general and his aide muttered something back and forth and then I felt the palm of a hand against my back—the general's hand, which made it an order, not a shove.

He said in that peculiar imperial growl exclusive to the top brass, "Okay, Hammer, let's go."

The older M.P.—a Negro with a scarred face and a triple row of ribbons—grinned back at me with his eyes speaking a silent language I'd rarely heard since the war. Not this Cold War, either, but that hot one I'd fought in, in the Pacific.

The other M.P. wore a professional scowl of indignant disapproval that represented a lapse in military discipline. But he was pretty young and had never seen combat and what he'd picked up about this situation might have thrown him off his game.

I shrugged away the hand at my back and stepped inside.

Originally, this smooth-walled, unadorned chamber had been designed for conferences, but from the expressions on the faces lining the huge oak table, this meeting was going to be an inquisition. And I was the guest of honor. The only thing missing was the rack, and maybe a red hot poker or two.

Tony Wale, Head of Special Sections, stood up, and with a barely perceptible nod indicated the chair at the far end of the table, the Prodigal Son's slot. Wale—tall, pale, dark-haired, looking like a top business exec in his Brooks Brothers number—didn't like what he had to do at all. Twice we had worked together and I had gotten his tail out of a hot spot, so he probably didn't relish returning a favor this way.

Eighteen pairs of hostile eyes watched me take the long walk down the aisle. I was a remarkably well-preserved specimen of a creature that should have been extinct a long time ago, but by some queer twist of nature had been instilled with instincts too potent to be erased, managing to survive into their pretty little world of appeasement and concession.

Somehow I knew that the older M.P., guarding the door behind me, was either still grinning or working hard not to, so I didn't feel too damn bad. Somebody was on my side.

I passed the four United States senators, the State Department contingent, and the high-level military advisors who didn't need uniforms or insignia to display their rank. They watched me with the cold, unblinking stares of nervous predators facing an unknown if natural enemy they knew inhabited their domain but which they had never encountered before.

One other pair of eyes watched, not hostile but betraying

nothing, belonging to a small, quiet, plain-looking individual in a gray suit and rimless bifocals.

I took the seat Tony Wale had indicated and sat down carefully, still sore from the previous twelve hours wedged in behind the crates loaded on the C-121. In one unintentionally comic motion, my audience all swung around in their seats to face me, ready to hang on every word, minds already dancing with accusations at the same time they were formulating their own finely worded excuses.

It was too bad my buddy Ralph Marley wasn't here to watch the show.

But Marley was dead.

And that left only me to play Scrooge....

Then the general pulled his seat out and, before he sat down, said, "Gentlemen, shall I summarize?"

It wasn't really necessary, but they all nodded anyway. Another group action. You could find the same shared expression of blank willingness at a Nazi rally or in a lynch mob or any gathering of frightened people who had lost something human somewhere and didn't know how to get it back.

All but that one little man in gray, however. Him you couldn't read.

And yet I could.

As he usually did, Senator Willy Asnet—big and beefy and draped in self-importance—took the initiative, a comma of white hair hanging on his forehead, part of that phony folksy persona of his.

"If you please, General," he said in his practiced Southern drawl. "We would indeed appreciate a briefing."

The general, who when outranked could take an order as well as any enlisted man, sat down, took a pen from his inside pocket and began to doodle on the pad in front of him. For some reason, the aimless motion of his hand seemed to mesmerize those nearest him and they watched his intricate patterns form while his words made their own patterns in precise phrases, couched in his commanding officer's growl.

"For those of you who are unfamiliar with Mr. Hammer's background," he stated, "I would like to supply the pertinent details."

His doodling stopped momentarily and he turned to a new page and lined the edge of the paper with numbers from one to ten.

Hell, I figured I was made up of more details than that.

"Name, Michael Hammer. Profession, private investigator licensed to operate in New York State, date of issuance of certificate, November, 1945. Military record exemplary, six citations, Bronze Star recipient, discharged honorably with five years voluntary active reserve duty. No prior criminal record, although numerous arrests for assault, manslaughter, and homicide. No convictions, however, due in every case to assertions, and sometimes pleas, of self-defense. Despite a reputation for vigilante 'justice,' his cooperation with civilian and military police and intelligence agencies is noted in his file."

What the general did not mention, because of its extreme classification, was that I remained attached to one of those intelligence agencies. An agency that served to deal with those matters that the F.B.I. could not handle because of its limitations as a domestic entity and that the C.I.A. could not take on because of its strict international mandate.

An agency that did not officially exist.

Even if one of its top people *was* seated at this table.

The general looked up from his scratch pad and laid his pen down in a rather grand gesture that apparently had some significance when he was addressing his men. Except that this time he was in the wrong company and nobody knew to be impressed.

"Mr. Hammer was admitted to Russia on a visitor's visa three months ago," the general continued. "We know from a tacit admission by Senator Allen Jasper that Mr. Hammer's role in accompanying the senator was that of a bodyguard."

Everyone here knew that the senator had suffered physical attacks at home by those objecting to what some would call his ultra-conservative policies. What might happen to him in Russia staggered the imagination.

"Excuse me, General," Senator Leonard Garris said, his professorial mien clenched in thought. "It seems unlikely that the Soviet government would sanction a visit from a controversial figure like Senator Jasper without providing its own considerable security. And why would the senator want private security when he could have requested Secret Service protection?"

Senator Asnet said, "I would have to concur with my colleague, General. Any violence on Russian soil, whether simple civil disobedience or an assassination attempt, would have created considerable international turmoil."

Garris picked back up: "Which is why I question how it was Mr. Hammer here, who has a colorful background to say the least, might be granted permission for this trip by either our government or theirs."

Down the table, between a senator and a state department flunkie, silently sat that little gray man who could have explained. If the agency he represented existed, that is.

"That would appear to be a moot point," Tony Wale put in from his chair to the general's right. "Mr. Hammer *was* given permission, and did make the trip, or we would not be here."

"Be that as it may," the general said, barreling on, "Mr. Hammer was arrested by the Soviet police and held in a Moscow prison. He escaped, slowly making his way across the continent to our air base in Turkey, leaving a trail of death and destruction in his wake, and smuggled himself onboard a United States Air Force cargo plane to this country... Mr. Hammer, since this sketchy outline of events is all we have, we call upon you to fill in the rest of the details."

Once more, like puppets on a string, they all turned and looked at me.

I said, "That's only eight."

Silence hung in the air.

The general frowned. "What?"

"General," I said, pointing to his scribbled-on pad, "you have numbers one to ten there. That's only eight. Or maybe nine. Depends on whether you consider my escape and flight one 'detail' or two."

Senator Asnet took his glasses off in that same deliberate motion he used when his committees were in session and he was about to chastise an underling or challenge a recalcitrant witness.

He said, "The point is, Mr. Hammer, that in the course of your escape, you killed forty-five men. Two were members of the Politburo, one was the warden of the prison, three were high-ranking officers of the Soviet military intelligence service, the others all officially detailed to either maintain your captivity or expedite your capture. *Forty-five men, Mr. Hammer!*"

"Sorry, Willy," I said with a shrug. "It was the best I could manage."

The senator looked as if he might choke, then recovered himself and glared at me. "Mr. Hammer, you will remember that you are addressing a United States—"

I didn't let him finish. I got up with enough melodrama and floor scraping by my wooden chair to make them all jump. Then I stood there looking down at them one and all, with that seasoned M.P. still grinning at me with his eyes. So there was one guy around, anyway, who would understand what I was saying. *Him and the little gray man who wasn't there...*

I made it damn deliberate.

"Willy boy," I told him, "I'm not addressing anybody. Not anybody at all. Try to keep in your superannuated mind that I am not under oath or subpoena and as far as I'm concerned, this is damn near a kidnapping. You yanked me off an airplane in my own country, and if you want to charge me with anything, try a hitchhiking rap... or using military transport for personal purposes, maybe. Think up any damn thing you like. You should be smart enough for that, or am I giving you too much credit?"

I leaned both hands on the table. I could see all of them and they could see all of me.

"At least somebody has finally asked me what the hell happened over there," I said. "My own government grabs hold of whatever details the Soviets are willing to hand out, accepts those as facts, and now I'm elected sacrificial lamb."

Tony Wale wasn't looking at me. He couldn't meet my eyes.

"Well, I don't play patsy for anybody, gents, not even Uncle Sam. I'm not holding still for a public whipping and if you want to try it, then go ahead and take a running jump at it. I'll bust this story wide open to the press and let them have a field day at your expense. Without any compunction at all."

I straightened, then grinned at them again. The silence itself was audible as these self-appointed Knights of this not-so-Round Table held their collective breath. You could almost hear capillaries popping under the skin.

The M.P. at the door couldn't hold back that grin any longer.

Something had gone through them, like a sudden attack of the flu. They all wanted to speak, yet didn't know what to say. Their eyes were bright little things focused on my face, then they stopped looking and started watching because the contempt I felt showed so plainly I could feel it in the way my mouth was pulled back tight over my teeth.

I was back in the middle of that incredible jungle of stupidity and self-serving calculation that was the political establishment, served by military minds who had never set foot on a battlefield.

These bastards needed a civics lesson.

"American citizens have certain rights, even in Russia," I said. "I wasn't given an opportunity to contact my consulate or Senator Jasper, either. Hell, it felt like I was in the middle of a one-man purge. And I wasn't about to sit in a prison cell learning to love cockroach-laced borscht waiting for diplomatic efforts to spring me. So I did it on my own."

Senator Willy Asnet seemed to be crouching in his chair, as if ready to pounce. "Mr. Hammer... your reckless actions have created an international incident."

"Screw it. That was *my* neck on the line."

Asnet came to his feet slowly, his face a barely controlled mask of anger. "You, Mr. Hammer, have put this country in an untenably dangerous position. Right now, thanks to you, we are teetering on the precarious edge of hostilities with the only other nuclear superpower on this planet."

"How about that," I said.

This time all it took was my tone to make them jump.

There was no respect in it, no remorse for what I had done, and no fear of any reprisals that might hit me. They looked at each other with a peculiar frustration because I was standing right there yet they couldn't quite reach me.

But they sure were going to try.

Asnet unclenched his fists and rested his hands on the table top, fingers splayed. "Your arrogance is appalling, *Mister* Hammer. And believe me, it will not be tolerated. This country is not going to be put on the brink of war because of the irresponsible actions of a single person."

"Really? What exactly are you going to do about it, Senator?"

His eyes slanted in an expression grim with the memory of the destruction of others who had dared oppose him.

He said, "You are correct to say you are entitled to provide an explanation. We *will* hear you out. Meanwhile, there are numerous technical charges we can hold you on until a decision is reached."

"Nice of you, Willy, to recall that Freedom of Speech bit that seemed to have slipped your mind. Oh, but I wouldn't try holding me incommunicado like *they* did."

"Is that a threat, Mr. Hammer?"

"You bet your ass, Willy."

He reacted as if I'd slapped him. "We may have to hold you for your own good."

"What's that supposed to mean?"

His smug smile did not detract from that grim expression. "That will be explained to you later, Mr. Hammer. Since you are well aware of the legal rights you enjoy, I won't press the point."

"No, I don't imagine you will. Not in front of this many witnesses. What's the next step?"

"Your explanation, Mr. Hammer. Your… story. We would very much like to know the circumstances surrounding your escape… and the details of how you managed to kill forty-five people."

With the deliberate pace of someone about to enjoy an execution, Senator Asnet sat down, his opinion already formed, the skepticism for anything I might say apparent on his face.

I wasn't letting him off the hook that easily.

I said, "After you, Willy."

He blinked at me. Like a half-asleep frog noticing a fly flying past his lily pad, sticking its tongue out at him.

I said, "You go first."

"*What…?*"

"I read some of the papers while I was stuck over there, and heard some of the Voice of America and BBC broadcasts… but let's hear *your* version of it… since you seem so damn certain of being in total possession of the facts."

A murmur started around the table that the senator stopped with a Pope-like raise of his hand. Over by the door, the big Negro M.P. was enjoying the show for all it was worth.

All those eyes were watching Willy now. His notes were beside him, but he didn't have to consult them at all.

"We'll start with the fifth day of November, of this year," he said.

I nodded.

"You and Senator Jasper checked into the National Hotel at three-thirty p.m., Moscow time. For the next two days, you performed routine bodyguard services, accompanying the senator to one plant, two museums, three restaurants, and the GUM department store. You accompanied him to Red Square to watch the November seventh festivities, and a Kremlin visit was scheduled for the fourth day. But on the evening of day three, at the senator's orders, you were to stay in your suite until he returned from a meeting at the American embassy."

"Suggestion," I cut in, "not orders."

He went on as if I hadn't spoken. "However, you saw fit to disobey his instructions and went out into the streets alone. One hour and thirty minutes later you made contact with someone the Soviet government was keeping under close surveillance."

I asked, "Why was this someone under surveillance exactly?"

"That particular individual was suspected of representing a foreign power."

"No kidding."

"There was an exchange of money and documents, and at that

point you were taken into custody, and removed to a police prison and held for interrogation. Before that could even take place, you broke out, killing anyone who blocked your path. In the weeks to come you hopscotched across Central Europe spreading mayhem until you were discovered onboard a military transport en route to the United States where you had smuggled yourself."

He looked up then, a bland smile tugging at one corner of his mouth, defying me to deny it.

"Whose version was that, Senator?" I asked him.

"Our people have been on this since the day of your arrest. It's the result of an intensive international investigation."

"Balls," I said. "Your people never knew what the hell was going on. They were always two steps behind me, and were never there when they were needed."

A bland, quiet voice from the other end of the table said, "Tell it your way, Mr. Hammer."

It was that little gray man, eyes placid behind rimless eyeglasses.

Asnet let his gaze flick toward this unassuming figure, annoyed, then sent his eyes my way again. "*Certainly* you can tell it your way, Mr. Hammer. No one's stopping you."

I grinned at him.

I grinned at them all for being such idiots.

The nasty grin with all the teeth.

"No," I said.

Both Asnet and the general blurted, "*No?*"

It was funny. Damn funny.

I got up. "I'm walking out of here. I have a business to get back to back in Manhattan. There's a man at the door who might be able to stop me, but he'll have to kill me to do it. And in that case, there's sure to be... what's the term the spooks use?" I let my eyes glide over all their faces. "Collateral damage."

Nobody said anything for a second, then the quiet voice from down the table cut into the silence. "Mr. Hammer?"

I turned and looked at him. Like me, he was a pro in the business, this small, quiet, nondescript-looking individual. You would never suspect the underlying toughness in him unless you were in the business yourself.

With studied casualness, he said, "Will you consent to a voluntary interrogation?"

He knew what I'd say. He could read the signs, too.

"With you," I said, "yes. These others, no way in hell."

Senator Asnet made a noise in his throat, as if clearing it to start yet another speech. But the little man got to his feet and gave the general a look, and the show was over. Some at the table were confused at the power this little man could obviously wield; others were in the know, the ones who shared a status classified at a level to recognize that nonexistent agency he represented at this table.

I pushed it a little bit. I pointed toward the battle-scarred M.P. "*He* can be in on it."

The little gray man named Arthur Rickerby nodded. "Agreed. But we won't need all this space, will we, Mike?"

All those eyes popped now. *Mike*, not *Mr. Hammer*.

After all, Art Rickerby was the guy who had got me my shiny government I.D. with its blue-and-gold card and embossed seal. The man who had once told a very pissed-off D.A. that Michael

Hammer's gun permit would be reinstated, no questions answered or asked.

And I was the guy who had delivered to Rickerby the Soviet assassin called the Dragon, killer of the valued agent who'd been like a son to this quiet little espionage expert.

Rickerby looked not to the general or any of these senators for permission to take over, but leveled his gaze at our putative host, Tony Wale.

"With your permission, Mr. Wale?"

Tony's gesture said, *By all means.* And he gave me the slightest smile. Had he and Rickerby been in this together, all along?

When I walked out of that chamber, it was a hell of a lot different from walking in. Some of those eighteen eyes hated me even more now, but in a few there was a burning curiosity and in others a little grudging admiration because I hadn't been willing to be the main course at this banquet table.

Nor had I been willing to chow down on their garbage.

This room was smaller with a little square table and four chairs. I took one of them.

"Good to see you, Rickety," I said.

"That's Rickerby." He took a seat opposite me and smiled the way a dentist does, right before he fires up the drill. "But you know that, don't you, Mike? Just can't help yourself. Just gotta rattle authority's cage, don't you?"

"Everybody needs a hobby."

Rickerby was a guy with unparalleled training in his background who had seen the tough stuff, and plenty of it, even though he didn't look the part. He had the M.P. sergeant introduce himself to me.

"Desmond Casey, Mr. Hammer," the Negro said, and offered his hand, which I took. His grip was firm but he didn't show off. "Call me Des."

"And I'm Mike. Too young for my war. Korea?"

He nodded. His manner was calm, and in this parade-rest environment, he seemed easy-going. But no question about it—this was a deadly man.

The other M.P. was still with us, his back to the still open doorway. I tried to keep a straight face and it wasn't easy when I asked him, "Am I in your custody, son?"

He came on strong, frowning, squaring off at the shoulders while his one hand inadvertently drifted toward the holstered gun.

"Affirmative," he said brusquely.

But the scarred-face sergeant said, "We're here to protect Mr. Hammer, soldier," chopping his subordinate up with his eyes.

Rickerby told the kid to go get us some Cokes from the vending machine, then to wait outside and guard our locked door, all of which put a perplexed look on the junior M.P.'s face. He was just not able to comprehend the sudden switch in attitudes—how had I managed to go from some kind of political prisoner to a VIP?

When the young man had gone out, looking none too happy with his lot in military life, Sergeant Des Casey grinned at me again and shook his head.

"Sorry, Mike."

"Kids today," I said.

Soon Rickerby, Des Casey, and I were alone in the small space, sitting at the little table with our Cokes. I let Rickerby use a hand-held tape recorder to take it all down for later analysis.

Rickerby sighed. "Like the man said, there's no better place to start than the beginning. Do you know why Senator Jasper took this little Moscow excursion?"

"Don't you know?"

"Actually, no. I saw to it that you were given clearance, when the senator's request came through, seeking to take you to Russia as his bodyguard. But that was the start and finish of my involvement."

"Till now."

"Till now. And you didn't utilize any of our people during your escape or the chase that followed. Over two months behind the Iron Curtain, Mike. How did you manage it?"

I gave him my most eloquent shrug. "I have my own contacts. I've done international work, and we have affiliations with private investigative agencies worldwide. And I have my friends in the press. You think my buddy Hy Gardner isn't hooked up?"

Rickerby's sigh seemed small but it spoke volumes. "The beginning, Mike. Why did the senator go to Moscow?"

"Nothing surprising. He wanted a firsthand look at the Russian economy. He paid for the trip out of his own pocket—he wanted to make a personal evaluation of how much their military expenditures were affecting consumption of civilian goods and the public morale. But, Art… this thing didn't start in Moscow."

"Where *did* it start, Mike?"

"Where it always starts for me."

Rickerby smiled a little. He knew.

"New York," he said.

"New York," I said.

CHAPTER TWO

The day had been sunny and bright, laying bare the dirt and wear of buildings, the age of this city as apparent as a fading beauty queen's morning face before make-up. But this was night and filth became subtle tones under artificial light and decay disappeared as if airbrushed away. Through the wall-size window, the glass and steel and concrete structures formed a geometric study with only occasional winking lights to indicate this view was of life going on in the city.

I was in the penthouse of the Wentworth Hotel just off Broadway in the upper fifties, attending a politician's idea of an intimate cocktail party, meaning there were over one hundred guests, with invitations required at the door. Senator Allen Jasper and his wife Emily had a chalet-like home in the Catskills, but because the senator's law offices were in Manhattan, they maintained this cozy apartment that took up the Wentworth's top floor. Just for convenience and entertaining.

Tonight was the latter.

No tuxes or gowns, just the kind of evening attire that few could afford outside the social register. I was circulating, avoiding prolonged conversations and the proffered trays of *hors d'oeuvres* and glasses of champagne. Every pop of a champagne cork, rising over the clink of glasses and the tinkle of Cole Porter from the guy at the baby grand, got my attention.

I was working security, of course, in a charcoal suit that might have been off the rack but was as expensive as some of the Italian tailored suits and Paris designer evening dresses around me, cut as it was to conceal the .45 Colt Auto in the shoulder sling.

A guy of my notoriety can have trouble going undercover, but tonight nobody had recognized me. Or at least nobody made a point of it. Anyway, I wasn't attracting as much attention these days. Just a middle-aged P.I. who used to make headlines, reduced to taking on jobs where he could find them. Like this one.

Normally I steered a wide path of political types. But I got a kick out of Senator Jasper—he was a conservative, a rare one from this part of the world, and he spoke his mind, which made him a natural target for the far left crowd and Commie front groups. He'd been attracting a lot of attention lately, not only in his native New York but all across the country.

Crowds cheered him, other crowds razzed him. But pundits right and left considered him a straight-shooter and a rare no-b.s. politico. He'd had plenty of literal eggs tossed his way, but never got any of the figurative stuff on his face.

The guy had humble beginnings and had worked his way through law school working construction in the summer. He was a self-made man, at least before he married money, one of that breed called rugged individualist that refused to go out of style but never would. With that chiseled movie-star handsome mug of his on that lanky Lincoln-esque frame, Jasper had no trouble attracting TV time. This was a guy in a position to influence public thinking—so much so that he might pop up on the ballot during a national election one of these days.

In the last election, I'd done a job for the senator, pulling the rug out from under an opponent whose people had gone for a smear job. I'd been backing up another P.I., Ralph Marley, who worked out of Los Angeles. Jasper had met him out there doing publicity and fundraising, and Marley had been on retainer for two years doing what might be termed bodyguard work.

I knew Marley going back ten years. We threw each other jobs that were out of our respective licensed jurisdictions. Whenever he was traveling with the senator to New York, Marley would call me in as necessary.

Like tonight.

Marley ambled up. He was in a sharp brown suit, the jacket just loose enough to hide the holstered .38 on his hip. He reminded me of Bogart in his heyday, if Bogie had been bigger and left his toupe at home.

"Pretty easy gig," Marley said in a wry near whisper. He also lacked Bogie's lisp. "Lots of good-looking ladies on hand. A hound like you ought to be in heaven."

"People have tried to put me there using a less pleasant approach."

"There, or the other place."

I let my eyes stroll around taking in all the smiling faces, the lightweight summer suits, the low-cut dresses, heads back in laughter or bobbing forward to make a conversational point.

"Don't think we're gonna get any clowns with placards in here tonight," I allowed. "But with a guy like the senator, an assassination play is always possible."

"What, some Lee Harvey crashing the party? Not with that aide of the senator's on the door, checking invites."

"Still. You never know."

"No. You don't." Marley smiled, then leaned in. "It's not violence that keeps guys like us in business, Mike. It's the threat of it."

I raised a shush finger. "Don't tell anybody."

We exchanged grins and he drifted off. We needed to work different sides of the room. Earlier he had pointed out and identified key guests—two army generals involved with procurement, Senator Parker from New Jersey, the president of Allied Servo-Electronics, all with their wives. Also, Warren Bentley, socialite and Wall Street genius, who was waiting for his date to arrive, Irene Carroll, the latest Washington "hostess with the mostess," who was fashionably late.

"The two have been making the social columns lately," Marley had said.

"If she's his date, why is Bentley by himself?"

"She lives here in the hotel, when she's not in D.C. Probably takes her an hour to layer on all that ice."

The Carroll dame's propensity for displays of Gabor-like jewelry was part of why we were on guard duty tonight.

Other guests on hand were typical New York partygoers, well-known but out of work actors, fashion models, bestselling writers, newspaper columnists, and society page escapees. Marley was right that there was a plentitude of pulchritude on parade, but the actresses were too obvious with their breastworks and the models too subtle with their lack of same.

One young woman—I made her for late twenties—stood out from the crowd. Marley hadn't identified her for me, so I had no idea who she was.

She was under-dressed for the affair and by that I don't mean her goodies were hanging out. She wore a simple light blue satin blouse and a navy pencil skirt to her dimpled knees and you could see that her legs were as bare as they were pale. None of this summer sun for her—she was as ghostly as that dame in the Charles Addams cartoons but not so tall and much more curvy. Her hair was carefully arranged to look careless, a startling mass of Carmen-esque black curls, her eyebrows heavy and unplucked, her eyes dark, her lips full and moist with blood-red lipstick punctuated by a nearby beauty mark.

She might have been Liz Taylor's younger, better-looking sister.

One of the temptations of a dull security gig is to glom onto a dish like this and spend all your time eyeballing her. I managed not to do that, but I did notice that she seemed to talk only to a handful of the others present—an older gent in his distinguished sixties with wireframe glasses, a mustache, and gray, thinning hair, who smoked a pipe; our congressional host and his wife Emily; and a gawky kid in an ill-fitting seersucker suit with a weak chin, eyeglasses with tortoiseshell frames, and a pronounced overbite.

That sorry specimen appeared to have accompanied this doll to the do. Was she blind? Did she have a nebbish fetish? If they ever brought back "Henry Aldrich," he was their man.

"Mr. Hammer?" The voice was male and resonant.

I turned and smiled at my host and his wife. She was a very pretty woman in her fifties who probably once had a great figure, but five kids later was plump enough that "matronly" was a compliment. It didn't help she was in a pink satin example of those nightmarish sack dresses the swishy French designers had foisted on American womanhood.

Still, her hair looked naturally blonde, her eyes blue, her smile radiant. We had not met. The senator was taking care of that.

"Mr. Hammer, this is my wife, Emily. She asked for an introduction."

"Senator, make it 'Mike,' and Mrs. Jasper, I am very pleased to meet you."

"Emily," she said, touching a bosom that had gotten out of hand, though there are worse sins. "I guess you'd call me a fan, Mr. Hammer."

"Mike."

"Mike. I've followed your... what would call them? Exploits?"

"How about misjudgments?"

Her laugh was another reminder of her younger lovely self. But even after all those kids, she was not hard to look at, no matter how hard the French designers tried. She had a sweetness that made you fall for her right away.

"Well," she said, "I followed you in the papers and just so admired you for... well, like Allen here, you're a man with principles. You stand up for what you believe in. You let the... what's the expression? Chips fall where they may."

"Cow chips, sometimes," I said.

This somewhat tasteless gag only made her laugh and she just kept rising in my estimation.

Jasper said, "We're both grateful to you for what you did, last election. You made monkeys out of the other side."

"Well, it was really just a blackmail scheme. Two of their boys are still inside, getting good at making license plates." I nodded toward the festivities. "Thanks for calling me in tonight. This is a nice party."

"Thank *you*," Jasper said, "for lending Ralph a hand. He's a good man but I'm hoping I can retain you on a more permanent basis."

"How permanent? I wouldn't take a job away from a friend, and Ralph is—"

"No, Mike, I would still travel with Ralph as my bodyguard, when his other work allowed. But when I'm back in New York, maybe you could step in."

"Okay. I'll consider it. I'm complimented."

"Does that mean I have your vote?"

"Last time I voted was for Dewey, back when he beat Truman, remember that? It was in the papers."

Emily laughed at this crack, too—she was an easy mark—then took my hand and squeezed it.

"You're a lucky man," I said to him, as they moved away to mingle. He smiled in response, but there was something sad about it.

"You're Mike Hammer." This voice was definitely not male, but it was deep enough to almost qualify. It was a purr. The kind a pussycat makes in your lap when you're scratching its ear just right. Of course, if you don't, you get clawed…

I turned to her.

She looked better than Liz Taylor's imaginary sister. Smelled better, too.

"'Evening in Paris,'" I said.

She almost blushed. "Am I wearing too much of it?"

"No. Just right. I sniff things out. I'm a detective."

She offered her hand. It was small and warm, the nails the same blood red as her full, sensuous lips. My God those dark brown eyes were big, almost too big.

Almost.

Reluctantly I gave her hand back, and said, "How is it a kid like you recognizes me? I'm ancient history, honey."

"Well, I'm a student of history. Among other things."

"Such as?"

She shrugged and black curls bounced. "I have a doctorate in physics. How's that for a start?"

She was already too smart for me, but that didn't keep me from wanting to play doctor.

"I'm impressed," I said. "You don't look old enough."

"Never a bad thing to say to a girl. I'm twenty-nine. Does it show?"

"Only in the right places. Okay. We've established I'm Mike Hammer. Who are *you*, Doctor?"

She almost blushed again and touched my arm, squeezing it a little by way of apology. "I'm sorry. I didn't mean to be rude. I'm Lisa Contreaux."

"Canadian?"

"Dual citizenship, now. I work with Dr. Giles. I'm his top assistant."

"I can tell I'm supposed to be impressed, but I don't know the name."

"Dr. Harmon Giles. The neurosurgeon? He was the top consulting physician on Gadfly."

The Gadfly space shot had gone off successfully last week.

"So why aren't you with him down at Cape Canaveral?"

"Well, because he's here. He semi-retired a year ago, but goes back down there as a consultant from time to time. He has a limited practice in the city. That's him over there."

She was pointing to the sixty-some pipe smoker I had seen her talking with earlier.

"I'll introduce you," she said, and took me by the crook of the arm and hauled me over.

Soon I was shaking hands with the amiable doctor, who removed his pipe from his lips so they could smile big at me. He was wearing a lightweight suit with a vest and a string tie.

"Mike Hammer," he said, and his voice was even lower than the doll's, with a burr in it, probably from smoking those damn pipes. At least the smoke cloud around him smelled like expensive tobacco. "You've been keeping a low profile of late, my friend."

His grip was on the lackadaisical side.

"Have we met, Dr. Giles?"

"No. But any Manhattan native feels like he knows Mike Hammer. I remember when you took out that Commie cell, what, ten or twelve years ago? Russian agents on American soil. They haven't tried it since."

Actually they had, but that was classified.

"I was sick for a while," I said.

"Anything serious?"

"Acute alcoholism."

This made both of them blink. When you speak the truth, it tends to shake people up.

"I spent seven years in slop chutes and the gutters outside of 'em," I said cheerfully, "but that's over."

"How did you manage it?" Lisa asked. "AA meetings?"

"Perhaps you took the cure at a sanitarium?" Dr. Giles offered.

"No."

Lisa asked, "What then?"

"I stopped drinking so damn much."

That froze time for about two seconds, then the black-haired beauty smiled, showing off slightly oversize, very white teeth, and the doctor chuckled around his pipe stem. His teeth weren't white at all.

He said, "You have a reputation for being a no-nonsense individual. It would seem well-earned."

"Thanks. So when are we going to make it to the moon, Doc?"

"One day," he said, eyebrows arched, "and sooner than some might think."

"So what makes a neurosurgeon a space consultant?"

"Probably my research work in the biological realm is more relevant, although the kind of physical examinations required for our astronauts necessitates the highest levels of skill from the consulting physician."

"Should I pretend I followed that?"

He grinned around the pipe. "As we enter space, biological concerns come into play. You mentioned the moon, Mike, but

Mars will be next. What if some organism awaits us?"

"What, a monster with tentacles and twelve eyes?"

"Perhaps. But perhaps a 'monster' that can only be seen under a microscope. Who can say? Dangerous organisms might even exist in space."

"Germs."

"If you will, germs."

I grinned back at him. "My advice to these space jockeys? Pack a ray gun, and shoot anything that moves."

"Ah. Frontier diplomacy. Manifest destiny."

"Some call it kismet, Doc."

That gangly kid in the seersucker suit came stumbling up with a mixed drink in either hand. "Lisa! There you are. Here's your highball."

"Girl after my own heart," I said to her.

"I thought you weren't drinking anymore," she said to me, accepting her glass from Henry Aldrich.

"It's not that I'm not drinking anymore," I said, "it's that I'm drinking less… I'm Mike Hammer, son."

He frowned and the tortoiseshell-framed glasses slipped down onto the bulb of his nose. "Have I heard of you?"

"I don't know. Have you?"

"Mike," Lisa said, her smile embarrassed, "this is my fiancé, Dennis Dorfman."

She had to be shitting me.

"How are you, Denny?" I said, sticking my hand out. The moist limp fish shake I got back was not a surprise.

"Actually," he said, tasting his tongue, "I prefer Dennis. That is,

if you don't mind. You can call me that if you want, but I just…
I never felt like a 'Denny.'"

"Okay, son," I said, and I gave his girl a look that said, *What the
hell are you thinking?*

She answered the unspoken question. "Dennis is quite a brilliant
scientist, Mike. He works with Dr. Perry Gleason, who's attached
to the organic science division of Manheim University."

"Manheim University," I said. "I've heard of it."

"Small but important," Lisa said, smiling, giving her guy a
proud smile.

Dr. Giles put in, "The government subsidizes some of its work.
Most of it in agricultural development."

Dennis said, "Dr. Giles has been good enough to consult with
us from time to time, gratis. A great man, Dr. Giles." This last
seemed odd, since Giles was standing right there and that sounded
almost like a eulogy.

"Pleasure to meet you both," I said, nodding first to Giles
and then to the innocuous kid who'd somehow landed the best-
looking dame here. Maybe she liked intellectual discourse. Or
maybe he was hung like a horse.

I let my eyes meet those big dark ones that seemed to be
laughing at me as she sipped her highball.

"We should get together," I said, directly to her. I was fine
about it if her fiancé wanted to make something of it. "But for
right now, I have to circulate. I'm on the clock."

Eyebrows going up again, Dr. Giles said, "Ah, so that's why
you're here. Security detail. But you aren't armed, are you?"

I unbuttoned the suit coat and swung it open just enough to

provide a glimpse of the gun of Navarone under my left arm. Lisa's big eyes got even bigger.

"It's all in the cut," I said, nodded to them all, and drifted away.

The expensively modern penthouse furniture had been moved to the periphery with some of it likely just plain stored someplace, making of the already large living room a space that could accommodate all these guests. Marley and I kept an eye on each other, and made sure we kept our distance. Each of us was glancing at the door whenever a new guest arrived. I'm sure Marley was wondering what was taking the famous Miss Carroll, who lived in the Wentworth, so long to arrive. Her and all her fabled gems.

I should have made the guy immediately, right when he was presenting his invitation at the door. He had an easy, comfortable manner, limber, loose, and a nice smile. Was he foreign? Anyway he was the only guest with a suntan courtesy of God, a small, almost skinny character with hair too long and a Fu Manchu mustache. Of course Senator Jasper had dealings with certain of the U.N. crowd. And this late arrival's tan suit was beautifully tailored, another Italian number, which fit right in and sold me momentarily. Like I said—all in the cut....

The latecomer made a beeline for the senator and his wife, who were standing with their backs to that big plate-glass window on Manhattan, attended by sycophants. A guest seeking out the host upon arrival was hardly unusual, but this swarthy character was moving faster than I liked, and Ralph Marley, closer to the senator than I, picked up on it too, and when the little slob yanked the Luger out from under his suit coat, Marley stepped in front of the senator, Secret Service-style, shoving Jasper out of harm's way,

Jasper knocking into his wife the same way, and the bullet meant for the senator caught Marley in the chest and my colleague had the same expression of surprise shared by civilian and pro alike when they know they've been shot, when they suspect correctly that they've been shot all the way, and Marley surely was dead before he hit the parquet floor.

I had forgotten to button my suit coat, after showing the .45 off to Lisa and company, which was a happy accident in this unhappy circumstance, and I was coming across at an angle with the gun already in hand, shouting, "*You!*"

The little bastard turned to me, spinning on his Italian heels, his back to the window now, and he was quick, goddamn quick, because as my finger squeezed the trigger I felt the impact of his slug in my thigh. My shot had been sent before I hit the floor, but when I did hit, I fired some more, and maybe he was dying already, but the stage was his, everybody had cleared away making it just him and that window at his back and I emptied the .45 at him, the window taking several slugs, spiderwebbing the glass, and he took the rest, the bullets punching a red-welling ellipsis in his chest, knocking him backward into that already compromised glass, which gave way, shattering like an icicle on cement, and then he was windmilling as he fell into the night, holding onto that Luger tight for all the good it would do him, and I hoped he didn't die until he hit the pavement, because he deserved to enjoy the big splash.

Then Lisa Contreaux was kneeling over me on one side. I could see Dr. Giles bending over Ralph Marley a few feet away. I had already made my diagnosis.

So it was no shock when Giles came glumly over, knelt by me opposite Lisa and said, "He's gone, Mike. He was dead before he hit the floor."

"I know." I felt slightly dazed. "What's all that racket?"

"Women screaming," she said.

"But not you."

"No," she said, smiling. Then she frowned. "You're shot, Mike."

"I've been shot before. It isn't much."

Giles was down there looking at the wound. He'd ripped my pants leg away from where blood bubbled but I hadn't heard it over the racket of yowling females, which was winding down at least.

"I'm going to give you some temporary treatment right here," Giles said, "then we'll get you over to my office and dig that slug out. It's not far, but we'll take a cab."

"Or we could go to the nearest emergency room," Lisa suggested.

"What, and bleed to death waiting three hours?" I shook my head. "I'm with you, Doc. Patch me up."

Then Senator Jasper was hovering. He looked pale as death, but he was alive, thanks to Ralph Marley.

"My God, Mike," he said, "how can I ever repay you?"

"Get me a glass of Four Roses," I said.

"So Jasper hired you for the Russian trip because of that," Rickerby stated flatly.

I raised a cautionary hand. "Let's just say it influenced his decision. He already had clearance for Marley, but like Dickens said.... Anyway, Jasper checked into me all the way down the line before he handed me Marley's job. Then the government did its security clearance number... ultimately through you, right, Art?"

"Right." He had the expression of a priest who'd been hearing one boring confession after another. "Mind telling me what he paid you?"

"Five hundred a week. Senator could afford that."

"What would Marley have got?"

"The same."

"Did he explain the details of the prospective job?"

I nodded. "Just a glorified bodyguard."

"You'd helped him before on that election matter."

"Right. What about your people, Art? Any dealings with Senator Jasper?"

"Our office was called in several times to, ah, adjust certain situations."

"And he always came up clean, didn't he?"

Rickerby agreed with a frown. "In the ways that mattered. Mike, it was his policies his opponents attacked. The man himself wasn't important."

"When a man takes the national stage, he is his policies."

"And here I thought you were apolitical." Rickerby studied his hands a few seconds, then raised his eyes to mine. "I'm curious to know why Senator Jasper used a private individual to intercede for him when government options were at his fingertips."

I leaned on the table and folded my fingers together. "He didn't want any connection with agencies that might have possible political controls dictating their actions."

Rickerby's eyes hardened slightly. "Mike... our agency doesn't cater to either political party and you know it. We've lost a lot of men in the field proving it."

"Sure, buddy," I said. "I know it... but I said possible *political overtones. That's the way the senator sees it."*

"Still doesn't make sense. You're a one-man operation, and we—"

I didn't let him finish. "The job didn't have long-range implications. It was a simple business of keeping him clear of any personal harassment on a glorified sightseeing tour. What little trouble we ran into was easy enough to handle. Hell, I've had assignments ten times as tough working with small industrialists."

"Ummm." Rickerby ran his fingertips lightly along the edge of the table. "You're trouble, Mike."

"Spell it out."

"You know what you did upstairs just now?"

"Hung everybody by their cojones," *I laughed. "They don't have a case against me, and neither do the Russians. I wasn't over there as some political hack carrying an attaché case full of state secrets. I'm nothing but a private investigator who was on a straight-forward contract job that would have terminated when we were back in New York."*

"Never mind New York, Mike."

"Is that right?"

"That's right. Tell me about Moscow."

CHAPTER THREE

If you had been flying from Chicago to New York, the nighttime view from your window seat would find the darkness occasionally interrupted by the shimmer of hamlets and towns below, not to mention the streaks of headlights on highways. But judging by the view from Riga en route to Moscow, we might have been gliding over the dark side of the moon. Then across the eastern sky came a glow as if of an enormous forest fire. Soon the silhouettes of the spires and skyscrapers of the fifth largest city on the planet made themselves known, though the sense of Moscow was breadth not height, its presence seeming to consume the horizon.

Riga—which had risen from the mist like a ghost of its former unconquered Latvian self—had been our first stop in the Soviet Union. We were a party of two, flying via SAS, the Scandinavian airline.

"It's either that or fly Finnish," Senator Jasper had explained. "The Soviet Union won't let any airlines from N.A.T.O. countries in."

When we landed in Riga, three paper-mache fighter planes were parked at the end of the runway to fool aerial photographers. Not a bad effort, but inside the minuscule airport, in a cold, colorless waiting room, an M.V.D. man in a green uniform took only a cursory look at our passports while our bags stayed on the plane. Think of the dope or firearms you could smuggle in. And here I'd left my .45 behind.

Then the senator and I filled out a slip of paper itemizing our foreign currency. Supposedly we'd have little need for cash, since we were traveling via Intourist, the official Soviet agency. The thirty-bucks-a-day Intourist tickets covered hotel, meals, limo/chauffeur, interpreter, museum entry and other public fees, plus twenty-five roubles for walking-around money—drinks, smokes, theater tickets. But I had five hundred in cash with me, because a buddy in the know told me the roubles-to-dollars exchange rate was high, and even higher when you offered greenbacks to Muscovites.

"Uncle Sam's simoleons can get you damn near anything you want in Moscow," a certain *Herald Trib* columnist had told me.

At Vnukovo, the much larger Moscow airport, the Slavic porters may have looked half-asleep, but they delivered our luggage to the Intourist lobby faster than I'd ever got them at Idlewild. As the senator's sole flunky, I was the one who asked the attendant about the Hotel National reservations, and was told a car was waiting.

And I'll be damned if it wasn't, a black limo called a Zi, which looked like a Packard circa 1947. The backseat had an oriental carpet, a clock and a fire extinguisher. Our driver was no cabbie—this was a militiaman, another branch of the M.V.D., and he wore a long blue coat with red-and-white tabs. He was friendly and spoke just enough English.

We had barely left the airport when an intimidating line of

tanks rumbled alongside us, also heading into the city.

"November seven," the driver said with a huge grin filled with nasty, crooked teeth. He might have been announcing Christmas. In a way, he was, since November 7 was a big deal in Russia, the anniversary of the Revolution.

Our driver was otherwise no tour guide, leaving us to form our own impressions of Moscow.

Like the wide boulevards, where taxis and trucks outnumbered private cars, and pedestrians scrambled out of the way of vehicular monsters like ours. Like traffic signals run manually by officers in a booth. Or the lack of big city sounds—no honking car horns, trolley buses moving damn near silently thanks to overhead wires, no loudspeakers or sirens from ambulances or police cars or fire engines.

Or take Moscow's skyscrapers, if you could call them that, twenty or thirty stories of ugly ornate architecture that at night hid behind glowing red stars and flickering red lights. Or the blocks of apartment housing that were bland echoes of housing developments back home. And no trees to speak of.

Why so many people on the street? It was after eight p.m., most shops looked closed, but families including swaddled babes were braving the chilly night in their colorless overcoats, marching along as if to a brass band. A silent one, in this city.

Jasper must have read my mind. He said, quietly, "Mike, living conditions here are dramatically over crowded. You'd come home from a hard day's work and rush into the out of doors, too."

But it was a clean city, despite thronged sidewalks. I was thinking Manhattan might learn something on that front, but when we arrived at our hotel, the first thing I saw was an M.V.D. man in his blue coat grab a citizen by the arm and make him retrieve a spent cigarette from where he'd pitched it in the street, making him place it in a receptacle.

Good thing I gave up smoking, back when I was drinking so much I didn't want to waste money on such a filthy habit.

The National was a mammoth turn-of-the-century Art Nouveau relic in the heart of Moscow. It had seen better days, but the lobby had a grand sort of shabbiness, with its marble stairway, mosaic floor, and stained-glass windows that were clearly pre-Revolution. Like Moscow itself, the hotel was antique and worn out in spots, but clean.

I checked in for our little party, feeling more like a secretary than a bodyguard. The desk clerk wasn't as old as the hotel, but it was a close call, a gent in formal black with a shaved skull and white handlebar mustache, on loan from a Tolstoy novel.

"When does the dining room close?" I asked him.

His English was simple but perfect. "At midnight, sir. There is no hurry."

Regular folks in Moscow might be overcrowded, but our suite was three times the size of my Manhattan office. A bellboy as ancient as the desk clerk distributed our bags to our respective bedrooms. I gave the old boy a dollar and he studied it like a palaeontologist who just found a dinosaur bone.

He bowed several times as he exited, saying, "*Spasiba*, sir. *Spasiba.*"

The senator grinned and said, "That means 'thank you,' Mike."

"I gathered."

Jasper settled down on a sprawling sofa, a Victorian museum piece that was more comfortable than it looked, and I joined him, giving him plenty of room—there was plenty to give. We loosened our ties. It had been a long day and we both needed shaves and maybe twelve hours of sleep.

"I don't believe the size of these digs," I said.

There were elaborate double windows, sealed with tape to keep the winter out, a grand piano, a nine-foot long brass-studded, green-felt desk, an array of Bukhara rugs, lamps with fringed silk shades, a stained-glass window of white flowers and bleeding topaz hearts, and several framed oil paintings, including one of an emir in Central Asia being attended by his harem.

"Princes used to live in this hotel," he said.

"Yeah, right up to where they lined them up next to a ditch and shot them."

Jasper smiled wryly and said, "Their loss is our gain. Ready to go down and eat?"

"Should we spruce up first?"

"Why, do you want to?"

"No, but I'm not a visiting dignitary."

"Nobody knows who I am."

"You want to bet? You think all Intourist chauffeurs are uniformed M.V.D. men?"

His eyebrows went up. "That hadn't occurred to me."

"How about those four guys in the lobby in black suits reading newspapers."

"So?"

"Reading newspapers at eight-thirty p.m.? You think there's a late edition of the *Moscow Gazette?* Get used to it, Allen. You're going to be watched." I lowered my voice. "You need to decide if you want me to sweep this room for bugs, or if you think yanking them would be impolite."

He was frowning. "You *really* think…"

I put a fingertip to my lips. "Let's go down and put on the feed bag. And let's hope in this country that's just an expression."

The dining room was surprisingly cozy for such a large hotel, with dark yellow brocade walls and lots of tables for four. The place was doing good business, couples mostly, overweight men with overweight wives in nice but drab attire. Younger couples featured girls who didn't need to lose thirty pounds, but they wore little or no make-up and their hair, whether blonde or brown, was in buns or braids. They looked like Heidi, if Heidi had breasts and didn't wear bright colors.

The English-speaking head waiter, who knew who we were and that we had just checked in, asked us if we wanted privacy—the practice was for guests to share tables if space was scant. I gave the guy a buck and said we'd like privacy.

"You will not be bothered while you are with us, sirs," he said with an obsequious nod.

This was a promise he would not be able to keep.

While we waited for the first of our three courses to arrive— fresh caviar, what else?—we were enjoying a little five-piece combo heavy on the violin doing an odd variety of tunes including the "Blue Danube Waltz" and a Cuban rhumba. But when they went into "South of the Border," a drunk Russian shouted out at them in what was apparently an anti-American speech, punctuated by finger wags in our direction.

Everybody knew we had checked in.

When the drunk weaved over, red-faced, and started shouting at us, the words were foreign but required no translation. I was just getting up to escort him out when a waiter, the first Russian I'd seen who stood over six feet, came over and dragged him back to his table, and sat him down hard.

"What are you paying *me* for?" I asked the senator.

He smiled. "That just shows you. Anti-USA sentiment here is very real. I think it'll be mostly in check on our tour. But it's there. Bubbling right under the surface."

"Allen, we've made a lot of polite conversation these last few days, but you've not told me what this trip is *really* about."

"It's a fact-finding mission."

"Sure. I get that. But why you? Why a staunch conservative? A liberal would get a warmer welcome."

His eyes tightened. "That's the point, Mike. I'm only going to mention this once, since you've made it clear our room may be bugged and we're being driven around by a militiaman and followed by men in black suits pretending to read newspapers."

I grinned at him. "Okay. Tell me once."

"The President himself suggested I make this trip."

"The President is a democrat."

"He's also the President. And he's an American. I'm not on any great secret mission, Mike. But I will be having some fairly high-level, unpublicized talks while I'm here, designed to show that Americans are not warmongers."

"I'm not much for appeasement."

"Not appeasement, Mike. You know I'm all for maintaining our superior military might. But war isn't what it used to be. It's not the shooting one we both fought in."

"You mean both sides can blow each other to hell and gone by pushing a couple buttons."

"Right. And things are particularly volatile at the moment, now that Mr. Khrushchev has stepped down, uh…"

"Voluntarily?" I said lightly, providing the word he was looking for.

An eyebrow arched. "Yes… 'voluntarily.' I'm here, in my unofficial capacity, to test the waters with the new regime. Is this Brezhnev character going to thaw the Cold War? Or heat it up? I'm here to help us start getting a read on that."

We both had the wiener schnitzel and it wasn't bad. Jasper had after-dinner coffee, which he pronounced excellent. I tried a beer, which I pronounced tasted like soap suds. Our waiter suggested a vodka martini and I took him up on it.

"In future," I said, after a sip of the potent cocktail, "I'm going to stick with the native drink."

The senator smiled. "The Russians call vodka a little ray of sunshine in the stomach."

"That's my new favorite Russian proverb," I said.

Upstairs I found the bugs easily—lamps and fireplace—and pointed them out to the senator. The bathroom was clear, so we could talk in there if necessary, with the water running.

But right now I took my turn with the facilities for an overdue delousing in a huge old cracked tub with no plug but a workable shower gadget.

This was considered a good hotel, even a fine one, and certainly Senator Jasper wouldn't have been placed here if the Soviet government was ashamed of it. But as I drifted off to sleep, under warm blankets, my belly filled with good food and a couple rays of sunshine, two thoughts drifted into my mind.

First, that this relic of a hotel, whose lingering opulence dated back before the Commies improved things, was the best the Soviets could come up with to provide decent accommodations to a visiting dignitary from the world's only other superpower.

And second, that all around this great city, its actual citizens were huddled together in far inferior circumstances, so bad that walking around in the chilly outside was preferable.

The next morning, after a breakfast of buckwheat porridge and diluted grape juice in the dining room, we found a strikingly attractive young woman waiting for us in the lobby. She recognized us at once, how I'm not sure, but she strode over with confidence for a petite doll of maybe twenty-five, and introduced herself as our Intourist translator.

"Zora Tabakova," she said, extending her hand first to the senator and then to me. "If you will please to call me Zora."

Her severe-looking black jacket and skirt with white shirt failed to disguise a slender shape whose top heaviness was all she had in common with the other Russian women I'd seen. The biggest shock was that this fetching thing wore make-up, her eyebrows shaped and darkened under a bouffant blonde hairdo—no braids or bun for this one. Her purple eye shadow made her brown eyes jump out of a heart-shaped face whose full, sensual mouth wore lipstick that made a bright crimson threat, or maybe a promise.

I guess my silly grin must have told her how jazzed I was seeing a pretty girl in this land of dumpy dames, and it made her smile, a big, gleaming smile.

Literally gleaming: her upper teeth were stainless steel.

"I have a schedule for you, Senator," she said, and handed him a sheet. "Would you like to wait in your room while I summon your driver?"

Her English was perfect, with just a little stilted taste of Russian accent mixed in.

"Please," Jasper said, nodding. "Just call us from the lobby when the car is here, Miss Tabakova."

"*Zora*," she insisted, and flashed that gleaming smile.

Oddly those steel choppers didn't take anything away from her beauty. If anything, they added an industrial touch to her earthy good looks in a somehow very Russian way.

She went briskly off.

We went up to the room and sat on the sofa.

"Pretty girl," Jasper said, amused by my stunned reaction to our interpreter. "Lovely smile."

"She'd look fine without *any* teeth. There are benefits to that, you know, particularly in pastimes where steel teeth might be a hazard."

He laughed at that, shook his head. "Porcelain teeth are damn near impossible to get over here. The last time the Bolshoi Ballet appeared in the West, the dancers who didn't want to defect were trying to buy porcelain for false teeth."

"So maybe those steel uppers can come out. Promising. But what about that make-up, Allen? That's the first lipstick I've seen in this burg. Is that hard to get, too?"

"Not really. Just frowned upon. A symbol of the decadent West, you know."

"Sometimes I think decadence gets a bad rap. But her arriving made up like a show girl means one of two things."

He frowned in interest. "What, Mike?"

"If Intourist sent her over dolled up like that, it's so she can get nice and cozy with us."

He was nodding. "Make it easier to spy on us. What's the other possibility?"

"That putting on that war paint was her own idea. Which means she likes Americans. Who knows? She may try to crawl in one of our suitcases and come home with us."

Jasper allowed himself a lecherous smile. "Would that be so bad?"

"Better than bringing a baby alligator home from Florida."

But if I was expecting a come-on from our beautiful silver-toothed translator, I was dead wrong. She was business-like and helpful all the way. She had scheduled us to begin with the museum inside the Kremlin.

"The Soviet government is anxious to share its treasures with the people," she told us, as we rode in our limo. She was sitting facing us in a fold-down seat. "This means all museums here are crowded. It is good to start early in the day."

Soon we were walking across Red Square, which was an oblong not a square, its bricks like big loaves of bread whose reddish color—not politics—dictated the name. Heading toward the Kremlin, I was struck by the soaring, ancient beauty of the place, its red walls with battlements and towers, the golden spires of churches peeking up proudly from within.

To me, the word "Kremlin" had always conjured menace. On this cold but sunny morning, however, it was just another tourist trap, with kiosks selling postcards.

And little Zora had been right about the crowds who were taking in such fabulous treasures as Ivan the Terrible's ivory throne and Peter the Great's ornate crown—school kids, foreign delegations, and wide-eyed peasants, all jammed together like the bargain basement at Gimbel's.

We took in an art museum, had lunch at an Armenian place, then spent the afternoon at the big state department store called GUM. It was a series of arcades, one on top of the other, selling everything from hairpins to fur coats; but the sales clerk used wooden abacuses, not modern cash registers. Without much arm-twisting, Zora had dinner with us back at the hotel. I was feeling like a third thumb, having encountered no situation where a bodyguard was remotely needed.

So far this was a vacation with pay.

In the lobby, Zora shook hands with us both, adding, "While you are visiting, I stay in the hotel. Should you require my service, call the desk and ask for my room." She turned those purple-eye-shadowed big brown eyes loose on me. "Should you need anything, do not hesitate to call. Night or day."

Back in our room, the senator said, "I think our little translator likes you, Mike."

"She's a cute kid. A guy could get used to that shiny smile."

We were on the sofa again, having some room-service coffee, which you summoned not by phone but ringing a bell.

"Careful, Mike. Haven't you ever heard of Baba Yaga?"

"No. Should I have?"

He was grinning at me, having a fine time. "Old Russian folk tale. Baba Yaga, the witch with iron teeth. Fearsome creature. But you should be fine, Mike."

"Yeah?"

"She has no power over the pure of heart."

"Great."

Before I went to bed, I went to the window that provided a fine view of the Kremlin. Dusk hadn't turned to night yet. This was what the movie people called magic hour and its blue shadows were kind to the old citadel's crimson walls and golden palaces. When dusk finally darkened to night, the Kremlin's towers seemed to flash with red stars—not an optical illusion, but weather vanes. Practical, these Commies.

I was under the sheet and two blankets and hadn't quite fallen asleep yet when I sensed somebody at my bedroom door. My hand reflexively went under my spare pillow for the .45 that I'd left in my apartment back in Manhattan. My heart started to work overtime, but just enough ambient light bled in to give me a silhouette of the figure.

A female figure.

Baba Yaga?

A witch with a silver smile, maybe. But a good witch, like Glinda. I flipped the switch on the nightstand lamp and it provided a yellow campfire-like glow. She was wearing a belted terrycloth robe, white, which covered all of her, but the hourglass outline of her was evident. The smile gleamed at me. Oddly, she had put on jewelry, several winking gem-studded bracelets, maybe fake, maybe not, but anyway examples of the decadence denied her.

"The desk gave me a key," she said. "Since I work with you."

"I figured."

She came over quickly, a little girl running in the rain, and sat at my bedside.

"I know I am bold," she said.

"It's okay."

"You are America."

Not American—America.

"No argument," I said. "Listen, kitten, you don't have to do this. There's only so much a girl should give up for the state."

"To hell with the state." She gripped my sleeve; she had painted her fingernails the same red as her mouth. "Can you help me?"

"Help you how?"

"Get out of this place."

"Good thing for you I yanked the bugs from this room. I left the rest active."

"Can you help me?"

I patted the hand that held my sleeve. "Sugar... no. I don't think so. I have *some* contacts in this part of the world. Maybe I could put something in motion for you when I got back, but..."

"It is all right. No strings."

Still seated, she half-turned toward me and unbelted the terrycloth robe and dropped it to her waist. She put her shoulders back to emphasize breasts that were already full and high with copper-colored areolae and reddish accusatory tips. The damn things were like the nose cones of missiles she was threatening to launch at me.

Fire away, a voice in my skull suggested.

But I brought the robe up around her shoulders and tucked the rockets away. She looked at me confused, and perhaps a little hurt.

"If I could ever help you," I said, "it wouldn't cost you anything. Not everything is capitalism in my country."

She began to cry, covering her face with both hands.

I edged closer to her. "Kitten, no... no tears."

"I am not a whore. But I love America. I love the idea of America."

And I guess I was as close as she could come to that—in Moscow on the night before November 7, anyway.

She flung herself into my arms, in a non-sexual fashion, though those breasts were heaving, and I patted her back, soothing her like the kid she was. Then she curled up on top of the covers, and I lay next to her, keeping a little distance. It was a double bed. Plenty of room.

"Pretty girl like you," I said, "*must* have a guy. Stay true to him." I just hoped the lucky stiff deserved her.

"I... I *had* a... guy."

"Had one?"

She snuggled closer. My arms were winged behind me against a pillow and the headboard, and she rested her soft cheek against my bare chest.

"I was young," she said. I almost couldn't hear her. "He was young, too, but older than me."

"What became of him?"

"Khrushchev sent him to Hungary. He didn't come back."

"Sorry, kid. When was this?"

"In 1957."

"No man since?"

"No man since."

That was a damn shame.

She looked up at me. Her purple eye shadow and mascara were smudgy, but it was kind of sexy. "You... you are a man who has a woman, don't you? Back home?"

"I do."

"You want to be true to her."

"I try."

"My man isn't here. Your woman isn't here." She gave me a wicked little smile, though no steel showed. Still, it was worthy of Baba Yaga. "Why don't we... make détente."

She kissed me, that mouth moist with lipstick, wide with passion, her tongue tangling with mine, and the steel of those teeth was cool, almost cold compared to the surrounding warmth and it was odd and it was strange and it was exhilarating.

Now I unwrapped the entire terrycloth package and she crawled on top of me like a confident cat, and I buried my face in those breasts as they hung over me like ripe fruit, nestling between them, then giving each the attention it deserved but only the hard tips and their surrounding territory could fit in my mouth, there was just too damn much to conquer, and when her head bobbed down below my waist, I heard the little clunk of that silver upper plate as she rested it on the nightstand.

I guessed those long-haired kids back home had a point. *Make love not war, all right.*

Special passes were required to get into Red Square on November 7, but the ever-reliable Zora Tabakova had them ready for us. The senator was in his topcoat and I was in my trenchcoat, the wind blowing little clouds of crystalline snow around, as we presented our passports to red-cheeked militiamen who regarded us with suspicion as chilly as the overcast day itself.

The Square today was hung with scarlet bunting and vertically displayed banners of Marx and Lenin, Stalin conspicuous in his absence. This sure didn't feel like Independence Day back home, and it wasn't just the weather—no children hung on roofs or peeked from Kremlin windows. The concession stands were limited to guys hawking coffee at a rouble a cup—in this cold, a public service. But there were plenty of people, all right, blocky men in fur hats and blockier women in scarves, brandishing balloons and bouquets and banners.

Zora got us in a good position to take it all in. We were facing the Lenin–Stalin Mausoleum, a flat-looking dark red stone structure with a modern look unusual for this city. This is where the bodies of Lenin and Stalin were kept on public view, utilizing some mysterious embalming process, maybe courtesy of Madame Tussaud. Thousands daily came to view the bodies—some out of respect, others maybe to make sure the bastards were really dead. We had seen such mourners from our hotel window, lined up four abreast, waiting hour upon hour.

Not today. Today this was a platform onto which the high pooh-bahs of the Communist regime, after a twenty-four-gun salute, strode out in black coats. The crowd cheered and more guns blasted, cordite meeting snowfall, tinting it blue. Soldiers, sailors, and airmen took up positions before the mausoleum in full military array, and a little gray car with a little gray dignitary rushed out into what I could only think of as centerfield. The car looked like a toy from where we watched, as the mucky-muck went around addressing each contingent with his vehicle never stopping, his voice amplified so loud it was distorted.

This was followed by a military version of the Macy's Thanksgiving Day Parade. The floats were traveling billboards of what I figured were socialist slogans, with grinning, waving idiots riding along, and that much, anyway, was just like home. For once, Russia looked colorful—young women athletes paraded in purple gym suits and bright orange stocking caps, their male brethren in yellow sweaters and blue trousers. Soldiers marched by, displaying more goose-stepping than a Hitler rally, though one platoon softened the blow by carrying little streamer-waving kids on their shoulders. In the background, brass bands and choruses fought for attention while tanks and assorted armaments rolled proudly, ominously by.

Maybe it made sense that they had allowed a hawkish senator like Jasper in to see all that hardware firsthand. He would go home and let his fellow congressmen—and his president—know that these Rooskies weren't kidding around.

But there was something about it that tried too hard. The military men wore looks of blank resignation not pride, and for all the cheering, I'd never been at a parade so damn joyless. And I kept thinking about those paper-mache planes on the Riga runway.

That evening Jasper was due at a meeting at the American embassy. Our driver would take him there and back. I was prepared to go along with him, but he raised a hand and said, "Take the night off. Maybe you can spend a little time with our cute little translator."

I wasn't sure whether Jasper knew Zora had visited me last night—she had slipped out before he got up. On the other hand, we *might* have made some noise....

"I feel about as useful as a screen door on a submarine," I told him. "Or is that tits on a bull?"

"No, Mike, I'm glad you're here. This trip isn't over yet, and not *everybody* loves us here."

After the senator left, I called Zora's room, but she didn't pick up. She might have been showering or maybe just stepped out for a while. Looking out the window, I could see that the snow had let up, and Moscow was quiet again. The November 7 festivities had moved indoors, where presumably a lot of sunshine would be filling stomachs.

My stomach was already filled. We'd eaten at what Zora said was one of the few first-class restaurants in Moscow, the elegant six-story Praga, where I'd had sea bass with a tasty sauce on rice and, among other things, one too many slices of chocolate cake from a justly famed in-house bakery.

That's when I decided to go out and walk off my rich meal.

* * *

"So *you* did *have a meeting lined up with somebody,*" Rickerby said.

"No. There wasn't any contact."

"You admit this young woman, your translator Zora Tabakova, approached you about helping her defect."

"Not defect. Escape. And I had no way to help her do that."

"You weren't meeting her?"

"Why would I leave the hotel to do that?"

"For a money hand-off. You made it clear that you might have smuggled in just about any amount with no trouble."

"But I didn't know that till I got in country, and anyway all I had was five Cs. Shy what I'd already spent, by then. No, Art, no contact. Zora was just a cute kid who wanted out of a stinking country. And me? I was just walking off a meal, catching some air."

"On a cold night like that?"

"Yeah, I know. Stupid, right? And I've had more relaxing *walks...*"

CHAPTER FOUR

Hands in my trenchcoat pockets, my breath like a ghost I was chasing, I took a nice brisk walk, even if my Praga feast remained a lump in my belly. Famous buildings were scattered around the Hotel National as if dropped there by a bored giant—St. Basil's Cathedral, the Bolshoi Theater, this museum, that art gallery. After all the pomp and circumstance of the day, the grand citadel of the Kremlin was asleep on this nearly moonless night.

Fifteen aimless minutes later I found myself on Arbat Street, once a main drag in Moscow but now a largely residential area. Here the quiet night was broken by the loud talk and laughter of drunken revelers spilling from bars and luxury apartment buildings—not your everyday workers, but party members, enjoying a better life than the rabble naive enough to buy the flapping crap on those banners at Red Square today.

When the black vehicle pulled up, I thought at first our driver with the limo had come looking for me. Was that the senator on the passenger side? Then I realized the car wasn't a Zi but its somewhat smaller brother, the Zim, and the guy at the wheel wasn't in an M.V.D. uniform. Nor was his front-seat passenger the senator.

Whoever they were, they sat with the motor running as two guys in black piled out of the back. This pair might have been Brooklyn thugs with their ex-pug's pusses and big bulky bodies wrapped up in big bulky topcoats, only instead of shapeless fedoras they wore childish-looking caps with ear flaps.

There was nothing childish about the nine millimeter Makarov PMs in their leather-gloved hands; those snubby-looking automatics could do plenty of damage. They kept a drop on me while their superior took his sweet time getting out on the rider's side of the Zim. Tall, imperious, with an Oriental cast to his features, he sported a gray fur Cossack cap matching the fur on the lapels of his black topcoat. His black boots had a military shine.

He yanked off my trenchcoat, checked the pockets, found nothing, and discarded it like a candy wrapper. He nodded at my neck and I understood he wanted me to remove my tie. I did, tossing it aside—the guy was pro enough not to let a guy like me wear the makings of a garrote. Then he patted me down, finding no weapons but taking my passport and wallet. Then he retreated to the Zim and opened the back door, giving me a razor-cut of a smile as he gestured for me to get in. Polite as a hotel doorman, which he somewhat resembled.

In Manhattan, I'd have the .45 with me, maybe even already in my hand in my trenchcoat pocket, and these refugees from a comic opera would be dead or bleeding to death on the sidewalk or in the gutter, depending on where they fell, and the guy at the wheel would just be a blank face behind a spider-web of glass with a hole between his startled eyes.

But I was in Moscow.

I got in the car.

The two-man goon squad sat on either side of me in back, their Cossack leader up front.

"What's the occasion?" I asked, just in case somebody besides me spoke English. "Key to the city?"

Turning ever so slightly, the Cossack allowed another razor-slash smile to decorate his oblong, hooded-eyed face. He appeared bored. I hoped I wasn't keeping him up.

"You are being taken in for questioning, Mr. Hammer," he said, in a voice as thin as his smile.

"What about, Ivan?"

"Perhaps you did not understand. A subject taken in for questioning does not *do* the questioning."

I was a subject now.

"Thanks for the clarification, Boris. You guys don't look like M.V.D. What are you, secret police?"

"There is no such thing as secret police in Russia, Mr. Hammer. That is just another Western phallus."

I think he meant "fallacy."

"K.G.B., then," I said.

No answer.

And that was it for conversation as I got taken for a Russian ride.

But if I'd been expecting the same as the Chicago variety, I was wrong. We were not headed for some remote spot in the country and a snowy ditch worthy of a Tsar. The drive was a short one, probably less than two miles, into central Moscow. I'd been working out how to handle these boys with their pistols on either side of me, but suddenly we were there.

In an area of the city given over equally to residential and industrial, the prison with its several buildings—this one gray, that one red, a stubby tower here, a tall turret there—seemed like just another rundown factory complex, albeit one behind a high brick wall with barbed-wire trimmings.

We passed the expected towers with their machine-gun cradling guards and scanning spotlights, but when we got to the massive metal main gate, it did not swing open for us. Instead the Zim rolled on by and all the way around to the back of the facility, where a wire-mesh gate in a wire-mesh fence yawned open, welcoming us into a parking lot about half the size of an A&P's. The Zim slipped in between a Volga and a Pobeda, two of maybe a dozen cars, all parked on my left. The driver stayed with the car—my guess was he was the Cossack's chauffeur—and was lighting up a smoke as they walked me across the cement apron, no handcuffs, just either of my arms firmly gripped and a crossfire of Makarovs pointed at me. Aging electrical enclosures along the brick wall of a low-slung building to my right indicated this was the ass-end of the place. The guards' entrance was my guess.

I managed not to grin. I was being carted in the back way, and these clowns were inadvertently showing me the prison's weak spot and the best way to get back out.

And I would need a return trip, all right, and damn soon, or I would be dead. I didn't recognize this facility, but I knew it was *not* the infamous Lubyanka Prison, which was where these K.G.B. boys by all rights should be taking me. That they *weren't* made this an unofficial detention, an off-the-books arrest.

A kidnapping.

But what the hell did they want with me?

The double yellow doors near what looked to be a garage weren't even guarded. To let us in, the Cossack unbuttoned his topcoat to make use of a key on a ring of them on his belt. For the first time, I glimpsed the Makarov on his own belt, in a cross-draw rig. The flap-cap pair hauled me inside, the Cossack shutting us in and then following us through an area where small snow plows and other maintenance vehicles were parked. We stopped at an iron door that the Cossack unlocked with another key from the ring on his belt, a massive heavy number that stood out from the rest.

For a change, a guard was waiting inside, a callow-looking kid in a green uniform with star-emblazoned cap; a baby with a baby in his arms, a very special one—a Shpagin PPSh-41, the classic "burp" gun the Russians had handed out like party favors to the Chinese and North Koreans a few years back.

The guard stayed near the door while we moved down a surprisingly wide, yellow paint-peeling hallway, so any thought I had about getting that burping baby away from this young-looking Russian was fleeting, with the Cossack at my back now and his two minions with their Makarovs on either side of me. I figured to bide my time and stay alert.

Not that it wouldn't have been hilarious if those two clowns both shot me with their Makarovs only to have each other's slugs go through me and into them. Still, not the kind of last laugh I had in mind…

This area was obviously not cells, and appeared given over to offices and locker rooms, though this time of night there were neither typing sounds nor the camaraderie of comrades to confirm that theory. Still, it seemed I really had been taken in through the ass-end of the place, which would make it easier for them to make me disappear but also gave me a shot at escape, if I wasn't walked too deep into this place.

At the end of the hall waited a locked iron door, and through that—the Cossack using another large key—we were finally in an area where the green-painted metal doors with food slots indicated these were cells. A few curious heads peeked out their slots at us, saw nothing interesting, then pulled back in like turtles into their shells.

Not many cells, perhaps half a dozen. This was a holding area. For prisoners who hadn't been processed yet, or maybe who weren't going to be processed at all.

Another red-star-capped guard in green was supervising this area—no burp gun this time, just a side arm in a snap-flap black-leather holster. At the far end of the hall was a wire-mesh wall-and-door onto an area with a barred window letting in the periodic light of a rotating prison spotlight, and the mouths of opposing stairways.

The Cossack stopped about halfway down this short hall and nodded toward an unmarked cell whose paint-peeling green was darker than the pale institutional shade around it.

The guard opened the door from his own key ring and I went in.

My new hotel room was six feet wide, four feet deep, its cot a plank of wood attached to one of the rough stone walls. That steel door clanged shut, then the oblong face with its razor smile filled the food slot, like the worst goddamned framed picture you ever saw.

"Do not get comfortable, Mr. Hammer. You will be questioned shortly."

I sat on the wooden plank. I had to act quickly and soon. My arrest was strictly *sub rosa*. There would be no intervention from Senator Jasper, because all he'd know was that I had disappeared. Same with the American embassy. I was a non-person now, like so many others in Russia. I was still breathing, but as far as my captors were concerned, I already didn't exist.

Busting out of this holding cell area remained possible. Once they had moved me to a cell block, escape became a much longer shot—not out of the question, but why risk it? Anyway, the signs were that they would attempt to get what they wanted from me, probably via torture, and then dispose of my American ass.

No, I would be checking out of this hotel as soon as possible, thanks very much.

Luckily their security was lax to say the least. For unknown political reasons, they had sneaked me in this back way, meaning I knew the way out. And but for that Cossack's frisk, which included discarding my necktie, I had not been closely checked. In an American prison, I'd have had my shoes or at least shoelaces taken away, and my belt. Not that there was anything in here I could hang myself off of.

But these had been crucial omissions. In my shoe was my five hundred bucks, actually in the sock of my left foot. In or out of prison in this damn country, dollars would buy me plenty.

And in my belt, in back, was the safety razor blade that I always carried, tucked in a slit in case some asshole tied my hands behind my back again. Boy Scout stuff, be prepared, but it had saved my life more than once. Not that Mr. Gillette could help me carve my way out of this stone cell….

But the Cossack was true to his word—I did not have long to wait. The two cockroaches I was watching were just in the foreplay stage when the tall character, still in his damn high fur hat and matching coat, returned with his two thuggish companions. The boxer-faced bully boys had their Makarovs out of sight now, but not out of mind: each had a right hand in a topcoat pocket. And there was also another burp-gun wielding young Russian along to accompany us through the wire-mesh door and up a flight of stairs to a door.

We were moving through a cell block, two facing walls of misery rising several stories joined by walkways prowled by rifle-bearing guards. Back home the guards were armed with billies, and I wondered how many times a guard in this clink got a gun taken away from him and jammed up his ass for a hot lead enema. Food for thought.

This was no American prison in a lot of ways. Walk through a cell block in the USA, whoever you were—Billy Graham or the Queen of England—and you'd get catcalls and the classic cup-on-prison-bars rhythm-section routine. Here the faces, dark-eyed and smudged with the kind of beard once-a-week shaves get you (*Look sharp! Feel sharp!* as Gillette ads put it), stared out in glum silence, faces of the resigned, faces of the damned.

We were on the slightly sunken main-floor walkway of this cell block, one floor up from ground, where I'd come in. Keeping the geography straight was easy, so far. But I had a big problem. Entering this cell block had meant going through a door opened by a guard in a bullet-proof cage. My best hope now was that between rounds of interrogation, I would be returned to my holding cell.

So whatever they threw at me I would have to take.

Then I caught a break, a real break. As we were about to exit the cell block, through another steel door overseen by a guard behind bullet-proof glass, that door opened and a small bald man with steel-frame glasses, wearing a black suit and black tie, came through and spoke to the Cossack in a commanding manner that belied his size, pointing back the way we came.

Their conversation was in Russian, but for whatever reason, we were to go back. That was fine with me, because it put me past that first steel door and into the less secure section of the prison. The commanding little man, who with a beard would have resembled Lenin, led us down the stairs and into that open area beyond the row of holding cells, where the beam of a prison spotlight made its swing.

The little man led us up the facing stairway and down a hallway lined with offices, the pebbled-glass panels of doors dark this time of night. But midway down, one door had no glass and was strictly sturdy-looking wood. Posted there was a surprisingly large brace of guards—three men in their green uniforms and starred military caps and flap-snap holstered side arms, and one with yet another burp gun.

When the door was opened for me, and I got nudged inside, this proved not to be an office exactly. It was too large for that, yet was smaller than a conference room. In the middle of the room a scarred square wooden table and four matching chairs might have been awaiting the prison bridge club. The walls and ceiling were lined with soundproof tiles, and even the back of the now-shut door had the porous stuff. The floor's thick carpet was the same green as a guard's uniform. No windows.

It was an interrogation room, but an oversized one, so it could accommodate the kind of watchers who in the States might have lurked behind two-way glass. But over here they either didn't have the two-way stuff or just didn't give a damn who the subject—I was a subject, remember—saw watching him being questioned. Two lumpy-looking characters in lumpy-looking suits with facial moles, caterpillar eyebrows, and hair sticking out of their noses and ears were standing there like they were posing for a sculptor making gargoyle statues.

The Lenin-looking guy bowed his head respectfully to them, said a few words in Russian, then gestured to the table, where they took two of the seats, leaving the other adjacent two free. Then the little man in charge gave the Cossack a look, and this somehow told the guy he was to escort me to one of those chairs. He did, and I sat. Why not? It was their show.

Then the big little man took the other seat. The high-hatted Cossack stood behind me, looming. His two plug-ugly minions stood on either side of the closed soundproofed door.

"Welcome to Butyrka Prison, Mr. Hammer," the little man said in a quiet, almost gentle voice, sharing with me possibly the least sincere smile in human history. "I am Warden Zharkov."

"What do you hear from Flash Gordon?"

He frowned.

"Guy in the funnies," I said with a shrug. "Maybe it doesn't run over here."

His smile returned, and it was at odds with his reply: "There is nothing 'funny' about this situation, Mr. Hammer. You are an enemy espionage agent, and you are in our custody."

"This isn't a K.G.B. facility, though, is it? It's local Moscow M.V.D. So why hold me here?"

"*We* ask the questions, Mr. Hammer. But I will say that in our government, distinctions between the local and the national are less…"

He was looking for the word, so I gave him one: "Distinct?"

Zharkov gave me the smile again. "Butyrka is a remand facility. You may be moved elsewhere… unless, of course, we can resolve this matter here and now."

"What matter is that?"

"Espionage charges. Crimes against the state."

"I haven't been arrested, Warden."

"In due time, Mr. Hammer. If you make it necessary."

I sighed. Then I gave him a nice friendly smile. "I don't know much about the laws of your country, Warden. I admit that. But I'm pretty sure I'm being held here illegally."

The caterpillar-eyebrowed Tweedledum and Tweedledee, sharing our small table, were just sitting there, watching me, showing no signs of comprehension. But nobody was bothering to translate, so maybe they understood English.

The warden said, "You are right, Mr. Hammer…"

"I thought so."

"…you do not know much about our laws."

"Then it's *legal* to abduct a tourist at gun point and toss him in a prison cell? Here's how *our* laws work—kidnapping is a capital crime."

"It is a capital crime in this country, as well."

"Comforting to hear, Warden. Keep in mind, in my country, if you kidnap somebody, you can get yourself executed."

"I know what a capital crime is, Mr. Hammer."

"Good. Because I am giving you fellas a chance to release me right now. You show me out of here, unharmed, hell—I'll even find my own way back to my hotel—and there'll be no hard feelings. No international incidents. Just a simple misunderstanding."

The warden was thinking about that when Tweedledum asked him something in Russian—apparently he and Tweedledee didn't understand English at that. The warden spoke to them for a while and they nodded as he apparently filled them in on our conversation so far.

Then, without referring to notes, Zharkov said, "In 1952, in an incident in an abandoned paint factory near New York City, you killed eighty-two of our agents and associates, and later murdered a prominent American senator who held Soviet sympathies."

The chair creaked as I shifted in it. "Well, those eighty-two agents? They had kidnapped a friend of mine. Remember what I said about kidnapping being a capital crime? And they were an ungodly mix of foreign enemy agents and fellow travelers, all on U.S. soil. I don't see that as a crime against the Soviet state. Just self-defense against it."

Even as I said this, I had a hunch a self-defense plea wouldn't go over as well in this country as mine.

"As for the politician I removed," I said, "his Soviet sympathies were secret. He was passing himself off as a patriot when he was in fact in the employ of a foreign power."

He seemed to have barely heard that. "Just three years ago, you dismantled our top execution team—codenamed the Dragon by your C.I.A. Tooth and Nail, a male and a female. The woman, highly placed in Washington society, you murdered."

"No. She took her own life."

"Not intentionally, Mr. Hammer. It was a death you most cruelly engineered. A trap you set. And you captured and disfigured and turned over to your people the male half of that same team."

"Again, Warden. All of this was on American soil."

"That makes you no less of an enemy of the state, Mr. Hammer. As you are on *our* soil, now."

He had a point.

The warden shifted and his smile turned sideways. "Regimes may change, but the soldiers who fight wars and the agents who serve in the shadows remain constant. You can perhaps appreciate, with your well-known..." He again searched for a word, and when he spoke it, he gave it a French pronunciation: "...*penchant* for vengeance, just how many of those in Soviet espionage circles would love to spend time with you, Mr. Hammer. To show you how they still feel, so many years later, about their fallen comrades..."

What the hell was he getting at?

"So it is in your benefit to cooperate with us," the Warden said, as if summing things up, though I had no goddamn idea what he wanted from me.

"Here's what I can tell you about Senator Jasper's trip," I said. "It's a straight-up fact-finding mission with some diplomacy stirred in. You've got a new guy in the top chair, our side wants to know whether things are going to get better or worse. Okay? Are we done?"

Warden Kharkov shook his head. "We do not seek information about Senator Jasper's visit."

"What then?"

"You are an agent of… what is your people's ridiculous, melodramatic term? *Top secret*, yes. Of a top-secret intelligence agency. An agency that operates in sensitive, critical areas where neither your F.B.I. nor C.I.A. can legally, officially go."

That was true as far as it went.

He continued: "We would like you to tell us everything you know about this agency. The names of chiefs, of agents, any active investigations, anything pertinent that might help maintain the balance of power."

If I'd known any of that, I wouldn't have given it to them. I wouldn't give these bastards any chiefs *or* Indians. But if they started pulling out my toenails with pliers or sticking hot glass rods where I'd rather not have them stuck, I *still* couldn't tell them a damn thing. Just the name Arthur Rickerby, who had given me this intelligence agency status for one reason only: to help him dismantle that aforementioned execution team, the Dragon.

And since the conclusion of that episode, my rarefied status as a field agent for this nebulous agency had served primarily to pressure the New York D.A. not to pull my gun permit or P.I. ticket.

The warden was still talking: "If you give us any reasonable amount of information, Mr. Hammer, we will put you through processing here at Butyrka—tonight you will be booked and printed, and have a full medical examination in our prison hospital."

"What's the point? If I spill, why not just spring me?"

"Because of your propaganda value, Mr. Hammer. We will keep you for several days. We will let it be known that you were associating with, *plotting* with, a known dissident who has been under our surveillance. But after a short period, as a show of good will toward the United States, we will release you back into the custody of Senator Jasper."

"It's a crock of shit. I never 'associated' with a known dissident. You won't make that fly."

"Oh, but you did, and we will, Mr. Hammer. And perhaps this will convince you that we are serious about our proposal."

The warden turned toward Tweedledum and Tweedledee, spoke a few Russian words, and Tweedledum nodded and reached into his pocket. He produced a handkerchief with something in it and handed it to the warden. The warden placed the folded-over hanky on the table in front of me, flipped it open to reveal the contents.

A sad silver smile.

Metal shining bridgework, spattered with blood.

I sat staring at it for a long time. Whether that was ten seconds or ten minutes, I couldn't tell you.

Then I asked, "Did you just torture her? Or is she dead?"

"She is quite dead, Mr. Hammer," the warden said, and I swung my hand around with the palmed razor blade in it and cut his throat, a thin red smile of its own forming, glistening into a grin.

The Cossack was moving forward as I jammed the chair back into him, shoving him against the wall, and his two cronies at the door were fumbling in their topcoat pockets for their Makarovs. I slashed the Cossack's face twice, one on either sunken cheek, distracting him, then let the razor blade drop as I yanked his nine mil from that cross-draw rig and shot both of his boys in the head before either had their own weapons out. Then I swung the gun up under the Cossack's chin and fired and watched his eyes go blank.

The warden was still just sitting there, grabbing his throat, blood seeping between his fingers. That cut might not have been deep enough to kill him, but the bullet I put in his brain did the trick. Much of what had been inside his head splattered onto Tweedledum and Tweedledee, whose eyes were wide and stupid under the caterpillar eyebrows, and who put their hands up in surrender. I shot them anyway.

The gunfire had been loud in the little room and the cordite stench here was as prominent as in Red Square today. Had the soundproofing been enough to conceal the six shots? Were the guards told to ignore little unpleasantries like gun shots during an interrogation? I had my doubts.

I up-ended the heavy little table, the corpses sliding to the floor with thuds befitting dead meat, and I waited for that door to open.

Would it open?

Finally it did.

One guard swung it wide and the burp-gun guard leapt in and I shot him in the head. The one holding open the door raised his Makarov and took a head shot for his trouble.

Then I was scrambling around the table and got the burp gun in my hands before the other two guards could rush the room and when they did, half a second later, a short burst stitched across their chest and knocked them back against the hallway wall and they slid down and sat under the smears of red they'd made on the institutional yellow, heads bowed as if praying. But they weren't.

Working quickly but keeping focused, I removed the key ring from the dead Cossack's belt. The big man sat there as if slumbering, the tall furry hat sitting at an undignified Tower of Pisa angle. I got my passport out of his topcoat pocket, and my wallet. Might come in handy.

When I left the interrogation chamber, I had the burp gun in my hands and two Makarovs shoved in my belt. I ran out of there, and halfway down the steps, I looked across at green uniforms and guns pouring down after me. A burst from the burp gun sent them falling over each other and slipping in their own and each other's blood, landing in a clumsy pile.

Up in the cell block, Russians were screaming things, whether prisoners or guards or both, I had no idea.

When I made the bottom of the steps, another gaggle of guards started down, got stalled by the dead bodies of the green uniforms gone before and they posed like a picture for another burp-gun blast, a pose they couldn't hold as they tumbled on top of their comrades.

Behind the wire-mesh wall of the cell block, the guard was running toward me with his Makarov raised to fire. I let go the rest of the burp gun's magazine and took him off his feet and the wire-mesh door off its hinges. I pushed through, stepped over the dead guard, tossing the burp gun and filling my left hand with one of the Makarovs. I remembered which key to use from the Cossack's commandeered key ring and got through the iron door that separated the holding cell area from the hallway of offices and locker rooms.

That young guard with the burp gun, the first guard I'd seen here at Butyrka Prison, saw me coming with the Makarov in my left hand and I guess there was blood spatter all over me and just maybe my expression was a madman's. He must have heard the sound of muffled gunfire behind the door at his post and he had gotten very badly scared. So scared the front of his pants was darkly damp. He looked like he was going to cry.

Had he fired that burp gun the second he saw me, he might have had me. But he hesitated and my finger had almost squeezed the trigger on another perfect head shot when he knelt and laid the burp gun on the ground as if in offering, raising his hands.

I leaned down, got the burp gun, and motioned with my head for him to get to his feet. He did as I indicated, and he understood when I handed him the key ring that he was to unlock the door for me.

He did, and was glad to see me go, and I didn't mind not killing that kid at all. It wasn't his fault he was born in this goddamn country. He wasn't responsible for killing a sweet girl called Zora. He was more like the soldier boyfriend she had lost in Hungary.

Call me a sentimental slob.

The sounds of gunfire hadn't made it to the parking lot, and no alarm bells were ringing or sirens screaming, so the driver— having yet another smoke—was just leaning casually against the

Zim. Unfortunately for him, when he saw me, he decided to go for his gun, and the damn thing was under his topcoat, buttoned away. He didn't even have one button undone when he died.

The keys were in the ignition and the wire-mesh gate was still open when I peeled out in the Zim. I was three blocks away, somewhere in Moscow, who the hell knew where, when the bells and sirens started.

CHAPTER FIVE

"It took a week to get out of the city," I said, "and start heading west."

Rickerby asked, "Did you have help?"

"You know I did."

"Be specific."

"At first, when nobody knew me, and I was just an American in trouble, certain people turned away, while others pulled me in. By the time the heat was on, and I'd been identified in their press, I'd been drawn into the anti-Red underground railroad. It surprised me to find how many people over there aren't in sympathy with that philosophy. I owe a lot of favors. One of them is that I don't mention their names—even to you."

"You said, 'By the time the heat was on'..."

"You think the K.G.B. isn't well-organized enough to effect a chase? They knew when they picked me up what kind of tiger they had by the tail. That bunch went into high gear the minute I skated out of Butyrka. I was lucky enough to have a head start."

"There must have been numerous attempts..."

I cut him off. "Sure. They knew where I'd head for. One team was tracking me, but others went into areas where I might well appear, and set up a net. I knew they'd work it that way, but I didn't have much choice either. I pulled every stunt I knew and got them to expose themselves. When they did, they got themselves knocked off. And I got through. Twice, it got too hot—it's not hard to out-number one man—and I had to backtrack."

"And despite all that opposition, you got out."

"That's right. I got out."

"No one's going to believe it."

"And yet here I am. I knew they'd cover the embassies, seaports, airline terminals and any other possible exit routes, and there wouldn't be a chance of breaking through. I kept my head down, moved from one friendly safe house to another, and survived half a dozen firefights. It took two months for me to make my way to that U.S. Air Force base in Turkey. The easy part was smuggling myself aboard one of our cargo planes headed to the States."

"You could have surrendered to the commanding officer of the base."

"What, and get taken out by a K.G.B. team because there wasn't time to set up security? Not this old soldier. I wanted out and I wanted out the quickest way."

Rickerby switched off the small tape recorder. He sighed mightily, as if he'd just set down a heavy load. "This has to be transcribed."

"No objection," I said.

He got up, went to the door and dispatched the younger M.P. to take the tape to its proper destination.

Then the high-ranking, inconspicuous-looking espionage

chief—he was definitely *not* an Indian—returned to the little table and sat back down.

Across from me, Sergeant Des Casey just sat quietly, his face an unreadable carved mask. Next to me, Rickerby was staring into his own cascading thoughts, the lines around his eyes deepening.

Finally, he said, "Mike, they weren't kidding in that conference room upstairs. This has the makings of an international incident that will make the U-2 look like shoplifting."

"I don't give a damn. All I did over there, Art, was protect my ass. I happen to like my ass, and I'm going to hang onto it as long as I can."

"You expect senators and brass and Pentagon think-tankers to give a damn about one man?"

"That man happens to be Michael Hammer, American citizen, and I'm here to stay and they and you are stuck with me. And so are those punks behind the Iron Curtain with their dream of burying us, and let them go running to the world stage squealing like the pigs they are because the action got a little too damn tough for them."

For a minute he gave me a blank-faced stare. Something was working at his mouth, like he had a seed in there and couldn't figure out how to spit the damn thing out.

"What, Art? What the hell is it?"

"Well… you're going to find it out soon enough. Your Soviet friends aren't taking this lying down. While you were on the run across Europe, playing tag with hit squads, they were sticking formal diplomatic protests up our tails and…" His upper lip tightened and some rage danced into those seemingly placid eyes.

"…and all we could do was sweat it out. Their propaganda machine went to town and made us look like a bunch of jackasses."

"I may bust out crying."

"Don't laugh it off. If you'd taken out a guard or two in the escape, that would have been bad enough… but forty-five deaths!"

"Not all at once. Half of that score I made *after* I busted out of Butyrka."

"Score!" Rickerby shook his head, his eyes wide behind the school-teacher glasses. "What kind of a man *are* you, anyway?"

My smile wasn't really a smile at all. My voice was a harsh whisper: "You *knew* what kind, Art, when you sicced me on the Dragon."

That stopped him, like a punch in the belly.

He had unleashed me because he knew I could get him what he wanted: revenge for the death of a colleague who had been like his own damn son.

So he couldn't argue with that. Then, as if asking if I cared for cream in my coffee, he said, "Do you know what the Soviet government wants now?"

"Why don't you tell me," I said.

"Their people must have monitored the call from that air force plane. They knew the moment you arrived back in country. And they know we have you in our custody. It's been confirmed through back channels. Mike—they want you returned to Russia. To stand trial for your atrocities."

That rated a horse laugh and I gave him one.

An eyebrow arched. "You think it's comical? They're considering it upstairs, Mike."

My hands turned into hard fists and the rage that started up my back made the cords pop out in my neck so hard I could barely speak. "Let those sons of bitches *keep* thinking about it, buddy. We don't have any extradition treaty with Russia, and if they pass one now, just so they can ship me out? Well, it'll be an *ex post facto* law and I'm not subject to it. The people in this country aren't going to hold still for that kind of crap, once the real story comes out, and the boys upstairs damn well know *that*, too."

"Mike…"

I jerked my thumb upward. "So tell the slobs to shove it— and shove it hard. There's no legal gimmick that can send me back unless I decide to go myself, and man… I've already *had* my Russian vacation."

He didn't react. Not really. He just sat there behind those bifocals and watched me rant, and when I was done, he leaned back in his chair quietly and said, "There's a factor you're forgetting about."

"Is there?"

"There is. A real cute one."

"Why don't you enlighten me?"

Rickerby's shrug was far more eloquent than my raving. "It's a matter of *face*, Mike. The Reds can't afford to lose any. They haven't got too much sympathy going for them in the occupied countries right now, and your little James Bond escapade made them look pretty damn incompetent, not to mention foolish."

I grunted another laugh. "What about that propaganda machine of theirs you seem so impressed with?"

"Well, some of their efforts backfired, and instead of making you look like a kill-crazy gangster, you came off one tough S.O.B. who wouldn't just lay down and take it."

I folded my arms and leaned back, grinning. "About damn time my finer qualities were appreciated."

Across the table, that put a little crack of a smile in the M.P.'s stone face.

Rickerby, however, was not amused. "Never mind your finer qualities, Mike. It's your neck at stake."

"Art... back off..."

But instead he leaned forward and there was concern in his face. "Mike, these K.G.B. boys are out after it. Your neck. The word's come through already."

"Back channels?"

"Back channels. If they can't get you delivered to their jurisdiction, they'll come after you over here. Whether they drag you back like a Nazi to Jerusalem, or just kill that ass you prize so much, it doesn't matter. Either way, they'll be big heroes in Mother Russia because Uncle Sam's entire apparatus couldn't protect even one tiny insignificant fly speck of a citizen."

"Thanks a bunch."

"After that..." He shrugged grandly. "...it'll be that much easier for them to keep their people in line. And we'll be the bad guys again."

The words seemed to spill through my teeth. "Let them try for me all they want, Ricketyback. I'll enjoy every damn minute of it."

"Settle down..."

"I got forty-five of those bastards over there, and who knows? Maybe I can get another forty-five of 'em over here. That ought to take the edge off their appetite for killing. Nobody likes dying *that* much."

Rickerby's smile was small but dripping with sarcasm. "That would make ninety kills for you, on this one, wouldn't it?"

"A nice round number," I told him.

"A new record. Forty-five and forty-five—like that big rod you carry." There was a touch of sneer in his smile now. "They say guys who carry big guns are compensating for… you know."

"Some times a hot dog is just a hot dog, Art. Why, you think I got a complex?"

"Oh, I think you're crazy."

I grinned at him. "But crazy in a way that's sometimes useful, right?"

"Not this time." He glanced upward, toward the conference-room gods. "Anyway, this time you'll be restrained, and we won't even have to haul out a straitjacket. There'll be no more gunplay, Mike. It's over."

"That so?"

"The men in that conference room have already arranged it— protective custody."

"Great. I get thrown in the slammer again… this time for protecting myself."

"Oh, it won't be all that bad. They don't have a jail cell in mind. They're thinking along the lines of keeping you on a military installation until this thing can get straightened out or blows over."

"In a pig's ass. We do that and I'm admitting my guilt, and so is Uncle Sam. Their propaganda machine will get it right, next time. They won't even have to bother sending their people after me. The longer I'm held, the better it is for them… and when I finally am released, they can line me up for a quick rub-out."

His eyes smiled with derision. "What do you suggest then?"

"Like I said. I'm walking out of here. Let the Reds take their best shot. So far they've lost anybody who came at me, and stand to lose a hell of a lot more. Maybe you haven't noticed—I don't go down easy, Art... and in every instance, I'll have a perfect case of self-defense."

He was frowning more in worry than disapproval. "I can get your gun permit and P.I. license lifted just as easily as I once got them back for you."

"Go ahead. You really think that'll stop me from packing heat? And when I advertise how the feds are hamstringing me, public opinion will make monkeys out of you guys."

Again he leaned toward me. "Mike, there has to be a compromise we can make. You're a problem, alive or dead."

"I vote for alive," I said. "Go ahead—make a suggestion."

He paused, thinking a moment, then laid his hands flat on the table. "We'll keep you under constant surveillance. You'll be free to do what you want, but if anything develops, we'll be right there."

"No dice, buddy," I said. "If I have a tail, I want to know it *isn't* one of our own people. You live longer when you know your enemy."

He recognized the logic of that. He tapped his fingers on the table top, thinking. "We're going to have to insist on *somebody* being there."

I looked at the big M.P., who'd sat through all our palaver in patient silence, and grinned slowly. "Do you trust the sergeant here?"

Rickerby got the picture right away but wasn't sure he liked it. "Sergeant Casey isn't trained for—"

"Like hell," I interrupted. "Take a look at those ribbons."

"That doesn't make him an expert bodyguard."

"No? I got served some of that fruit salad myself. They don't just hand that stuff out on the buffet line. They give those to you for being able to fight and kill, to out-think the enemy and stay alive when the shit storm comes."

Rickerby turned and looked at the M.P. "Opinion, Sergeant? This would be strictly voluntary."

The sergeant's grin was broad and flat, with humor in his eyes; but behind the smile there was something else and I liked what I saw.

He said, "Sounds like great duty, sir."

Rickerby lifted both eyebrows, sighed, then gestured with open hands. "We'll give it a try, then."

The M.P.'s smile was gone, his expression serious, almost somber now. "Sir…"

"Yes?"

"I wouldn't worry too much about my qualifications. After the war I spent six years on the NYPD. Made detective."

A grin stretched across my mouth. "Why'd you go back to the service?"

He made a gesture with his shoulders and grinned back. "It felt more like home to me."

Good man.

Rickerby said, "Mike, I've made one hell of a concession to you. And I have to sell it to the men upstairs."

"And you need something from me."

He nodded. "The transcription of my interview with you will be gone over and gone over again… and they are going to have their own questions. They'll have a desire for verification of certain details."

"To be expected."

"I'll be right there and won't let them overstep."

"Neither will I, Art."

They gave me guest quarters fit for a five-star general, with five-star room service to boot. I put away a prime rib dinner with all the trimmings, and got a big kick out of spending an evening watching television that wasn't in black-and-white and Russian. Before bed I took a hot shower that made me proud to be an American, and then slept like a baby for the first time in months.

Des Casey had the room next door, so his bodyguard job had already begun. Me with a bodyguard—that was rich. But I might come to appreciate having the extra firepower and know-how. Right now, however, I didn't figure the K.G.B. would be storming the Pentagon….

The next morning, the press room was packed with reporters waiting impatiently for a story to feed their millions. They weren't happy having hours to wait before getting access to me. And I wasn't happy, either. But this was Rickerby's price and I had to pay it.

First, the brain pickers had to scan every detail in that transcript. They did so in a room wired for recording while 16mm film cameras captured my reactions. Rickerby had asked if I'd submit to a polygraph during questioning and I said no problem. This acquiescence to scientific scrutiny surprised the specialists, who had likely been told what a pain in the ass I was.

For forty minutes they examined my background, checking the polygraph responses against my records, then brought things right up to date with the Russian incident. Senator Jasper had submitted his report about hiring me and what little he knew of the situation, and I could tell by their faces that it tallied with my own account.

With each answer, I could see, ever so slightly, frustration and annoyance touch their expressions. Not that they weren't pros— they approached my story from every angle in obtuse ways that would have tripped up anybody trying to cover up. But I wasn't trying to cover up. I didn't have to.

At eleven-thirty, we took a half-hour break, then they hooked me back up to the gizmo again. A fresh interrogator took the seat behind the desk while the others stood by quietly in their lab coats, clipboards in hand.

I tried to keep my answers civil, but when I was asked about the necessity of responding to my captivity in "such a violent fashion," I let loose.

"All I knew was I was being set up as a target," I said, "and my death day was right there and then. I wasn't interested in niceties. I just got my ass out as fast as I could, and if you don't like it, you know where to stick it."

This time the polygraph registered more than simple fluctuations. The needle scratched angrily, almost exceeding the limitations of the graph, and still pulsated with the emotions inside me after I'd stopped talking.

From the sidelines, Rickerby ordered, "Cut it off," and hands unfastened the attachments that had made me a part of the machine.

We waited in a small break room for the questioners to analyze their findings. Coffee and sandwiches were available in vending machines. Not five-star but welcome. Des guarded the door from out in the hall.

Rickerby sipped coffee and his smile was genuine if weary. "You just can't cut us any slack, can you, Mike?"

"Sorry, kid. I did my best. You know me—when they push the right button…"

"The press corps may push your buttons, too. They're waiting for your story right now. How are you going to handle that?"

"With the truth."

"I guess the truth will have to do," he said. "You're something of a celebrity again, you know. How many comebacks does this make?"

"Who's counting?"

Rickerby seemed ill at ease suddenly. "Mike, I… I appreciate that you covered for my intelligence group, under that Russian questioning."

"For a card-carrying member, I didn't have that much to spill."

"You could have given them my name."

"Naw. That wouldn't happen."

"They might have tortured you."

"Art, they can't torture you if you kill them first."

He laughed. Actually laughed. "You do have a point of view all your own, Mike. But do you think this could have been about something else? Other than getting intel out of you about my group? Or striking back at you because of the 1952 incident? Or the Dragon...?"

"Like what?"

"Like maybe someplace you came across something. On some seemingly unrelated job."

"Art," I said, "don't you think I haven't been over that angle? Hell, man, I've relived every minute of every case the past few years and I can't tie in anything. Since the Dragon, there's been nothing related to international events."

He turned over a hand. "The polygraph supports what you say, and I'm confident when they break down your statement, the experts will come to the same conclusion."

I had a bite of ham sandwich. "Then there's nothing more to it than what the warden of Butyrka questioned me about."

"Possibly. Of course... there's that *other* angle."

"What other angle?"

He seemed hesitant even to say it. "...Velda."

Velda, my secretary. Velda, my partner. Velda, my love. Velda who had worked with me at Hammer Investigations from the beginning, who carried her own P.I. ticket, who had worked vice for the NYPD; but before that, during the war, had been in the O.S.I. and the O.S.S., an impossibly young, impossibly beautiful agent, who years later got unexpectedly drawn back into the espionage game. Who for seven drunken years I had thought dead, when in reality she had been behind the Iron Curtain, desperately trying to stay alive even as she served her country, called back to service by fate and circumstance but answering that call because she was, in her way, a patriot. A patriot spending seven long years on a mission that had come out of the past to swallow her up, making my two months behind that same Iron Curtain seem like a guided tour, and when she finally came home to me, after I played St. George to the Dragon that had sought to slay her, she had told Art Rickerby and his people everything she had learned about the deadliest espionage ring on earth, and in Moscow thirty men died and in the East Zone of Berlin five more disappeared and the tremors were felt across the face of the globe.

Rickerby's eyes were unblinking. "Nothing small about what Velda did over there, Mike. And her experience was similar to yours."

"She had it so much tougher…"

"Well? What about it?"

I shook my head. "I don't buy a connection. That warden, that guy Zharkov, when he was going over my past sins, never mentioned her. There's been a regime change since then. Hell, what she did may have helped pave the way for it."

His eyebrows were up. "I doubt they think she's due a medal."

"Come on, Art, you know these political affairs wash themselves out. When they're over, they're over. And anyway, when this Jasper thing came up, she was out of town. For two months before I left, she'd been down in Miami on the Dixon-Mays case. Cummings Insurance hired us directly to get inside the thing."

Rickerby was nodding. "I know about that. We talked to her a number of times while you were M.I.A. She handled herself well, as you might expect… and she seems to have run your agency just fine without you around."

"If that's supposed to be a needle, forget it. Nobody has a

higher opinion of Velda's abilities than me."

Des Casey stuck his head in the break room and called Rickerby out into the hall. Minutes later, the intelligence chief returned to say, "They're going to spring you."

"Nice of them."

"The press has been asked to play it down. They'll be given a condensed, softened version of your statement and we'll try to minimize the situation. You'll be fully briefed before you go out there. On your own, you'll have to be careful of freelance writers going for the sensational, and stay on your toes with the regular press. They've okayed your sergeant friend to accompany you until we think you're clear to go back to whatever your version of a normal life might be. In the meantime, and this is not negotiable, a few security men from Special Sections will be spotted around."

I frowned. "Will they know the chance they're taking? A tail to me means one thing, Art, and I'm not going to ask for identification if somebody moves the wrong way."

Rickerby smiled faintly and nodded. "Please, Mike. They've been around, too."

"It'll be your headache, buddy. Who's my contact?"

"Me. Any time at all. At the usual stand."

That was an address as nondescript as Rickerby himself— Peerless Brokers on Broadway.

"Am I still in business, Art?"

"Certainly," he said. "Even Mike Hammer has to make a living. We'd hate for you to wind up on welfare. Besides, all this publicity should be good for business."

"Doesn't matter. I already have a case."

That surprised him. "What could that be, after a two-month hiatus?"

"*This* case, Art. This case right here."

"There *is* no case. There's just you trying to stay alive if the K.G.B. comes calling."

I shook my head. "That's just the sidebar. The headline story is the murders."

"What murders?"

"Of a great guy named Ralph Marley here in America, and a lovely young Russian with a memorable smile called Zora Tabakova."

Rickerby was looking at me the way a traffic cop looks at a bad accident. "You shot Marley's killer and sent him hurtling twelve stories to the pavement. And how are you going to avenge that little translator? Didn't you already kill forty-five goddamn Reds?"

"It's a start," I allowed.

I wasn't exactly unknown to the members of the Fourth Estate. They read the government handouts diligently but with a grain of salt, knowing there was more to the story but willing to cooperate from a security standpoint. Too many of them gave me that peculiar stare, wondering when the next phase would begin, their minds automatically formulating a lead or an obit. Most were on my side already and I caught the half-hidden "see-you-later" gestures they passed my way.

My own statement only verified the handouts, suggesting that the fault lay with the Russian authorities who had abducted me and denied me contact with the American embassy and who therefore took their chances should I choose to seek my God-given freedom.

I was now back on native soil (I reminded them) and under the protection of the U.S. Government, and any official or non-official action by the Soviet government to take recourse would be looked upon as an unfriendly act. In the meantime, the proper agencies would investigate thoroughly and give a detailed report to Congress, and the Soviet delegation.

No mention was made of Sergeant Desmond Casey or the details of the events I'd outlined. The lid was on and on tight. I walked out with Casey, who was now in street clothes, and took the north corridor to where they had a car waiting, and drove out to the airport.

An hour and a half later, I was in New York telling a cabbie to take me to my office, then sitting back wearing a big shit-eating grin as I glanced at the brawny Negro sergeant beside me.

Both of us had spotted the squat guy in the gray suit who took the same shuttle plane we did, and right now was fifty yards behind us in another taxi.

But I was going to let him come to me.

CHAPTER SIX

By the time we hit the East Side Drive, we had it planned out.

I gave the cabbie a slightly circuitous route, just to make sure our tail was sticking with us. Then I directed him to a corner near a hotel where I knew cabs would be waiting.

We pulled over and Des Casey climbed out, making an elaborate show out of saying so long, and heading into the hotel. I went on alone in the cab. Behind me, the squat guy's hack had paused half a block behind, and now took up my tail, apparently secure in the cover the other cabs were lending.

But it was a damn near sure bet our squat pal's hackie didn't notice Casey slip back out and catch a cab behind him, falling in line on our little caravan.

My cabbie, a Puerto Rican in his twenties, pulled up in front of the Hackard Building. I leaned up and passed him a ten. His grin was blazing white in his brown face.

"You're Mike Hammer, ain't you, man?"

"I used to be," I admitted. "Keep it."

"I should have you sign it, man. Frame the damn thing."

"Naw. Buy the baby some grub."

"How you know I'm a new papa, man?"

Little knitted blue baby shoes were hanging off his rear-view mirror.

"I'm a detective," I said.

My office was on the eighth floor of the old building, which had seen better days and was overdue a renovation. I had that odd feeling you get when you return to the familiar after a long while away—a mingling of comfort and apprehension. As I stood in the lobby waiting for the elevator doors to open, I thought about how she was up there, waiting for me, business as usual. And yet there was nothing about Velda that was "usual."

It had been a long, long time away from her, a hungry time, often a desperate time, wondering if the odds were so long that seeing her even once more was too much to dare hope for...

At 808, I turned the knob gently and eased the door open, stepped inside, and closed it silently. The outer office was empty, but the roses I'd had sent to her were in a vase on her desk. I smiled.

My inner office door was open and I found her standing behind my desk, a hand on my chair as if on my shoulder, her back to me, staring out the window into a blazing sunset that was pulling a dark curtain over the city. The black velvet of her hair made a beautiful torrent spilling down over her shoulders, filtering the fading light. She wore a cream-colored silk blouse separated from a dark brown skirt by a wide tan belt, such a simple ensemble and yet they served so well the strength and loveliness of a tall, full-breasted body reflected in the width of her shoulders, the narrowness of her waist, and the athletic grace of her posture.

I said, "Hello, Velda," and she turned around slowly, her deep brown eyes wide for a bare instant, a smile taut with concern blossoming into one of pure joy in the microsecond that she saw I was really there and alive and smiling at her.

"Mike…"

She didn't have to say anything more. That was enough. She came to me and I came to her and she was in my arms, one big bundle of love that exploded against me in tears and sobs of pleasure and relief, her mouth searching for mine in a frenzy of passion.

I held her away and looked at her, not able to do anything more than give her a silly grin. "You're slipping. I didn't think anybody could sneak up on you."

Her full, sensuous mouth managed to go pixie-ish in a smile as she lifted her right hand and let me glimpse the little .32 nestled in her lady-like palm.

I laughed and said, "It's great to be home, kid."

"Oh, Mike, you idiot. You great big jerk. How long have you been in country?"

"Yesterday."

"And you didn't call?"

"I was under a sort of house arrest. A little hotel called the Pentagon. I think it's one of the Hilton chain."

"Jokes. Your face…" She touched it here, and here, and there. "Some new scars… That's a new trenchcoat, too, isn't it? What, Burberry? And a new suit?"

"Yeah. They decked me out before they showed me off to the press. What I turned up in wasn't that presentable."

"I'm so glad you're in one piece."

"Why, didn't you think I'd make it?"

Velda wiped her eyes with the side of a fist and let a laugh take over. "I knew you'd make it. I bet on you. Literally. There are people who're going to owe me money tomorrow."

"I'm glad somebody had confidence in me."

"Couldn't you have called? Couldn't you have written? No. I'm sorry. Forget I said that. I'm no one to talk."

Her jaunt behind the Iron Curtain had lasted seven years, after all.

"Just getting those flowers ordered," I said, "was a small miracle."

"You didn't sign the card."

"No. Everything's top secret where they had me."

We walked out into the outer office, I hung up my hat and trenchcoat, and we sat on the couch.

I said, "I just couldn't risk contact while I was over there, kitten. I didn't want my location pinpointed. They would have expected that and had the mail covered, and phones were out of the question. That damn country is a mix of peasantry out of the middle ages and technology out of science fiction. No, I wasn't about to take any chances."

Velda nodded. "I know. And I understood. At least we knew you were alive, from the stories coming out of TASS and *Pravda*. I've saved the clippings."

"Great. Make a scrapbook out of them and give them to me for Christmas in thirty years."

She was sitting sideways on the couch, her skirt above her

knees. Her legs were long and muscular and tan. I was a damn fool for ever looking at any other woman.

"And now," she said, eyebrows high, "can you please tell me all about it before I bust?"

I pulled her in close to me and nuzzled the side of her neck. "Why don't I bust *you*," I whispered. "In the mouth..." I put a hand on a full, silk-covered breast and the nub of a nipple poked back at me. "Or why don't you bust *me*..."

She laughed lightly, pushed me away, and leaned her head back with that playful superiority a lovely woman can wield over a guy. "Later, Tarzan. Tell me the story first."

"I'll buy you a paper. I gave a press conference and it should be in the late edition."

"I'll take the uncensored version, if you don't mind."

It took half an hour to tell the story, though I did censor aspects having to do with the late Zora. We had an understanding, Velda and I—I could sow wild oats until I was ready to marry her, as long as I didn't bring home any big diseases or little bastards.

Anyway, we went through half a pot of coffee as I gave her chapter and verse, and she was narrow-eyed and intense, as she took it in, asking only occasional pertinent questions when I skipped or blurred over something.

When I finished, she immediately pointed out the incongruity of it all.

"A capture, an escape, a chase," she said. "And the K.G.B., or anyway their masters, risked the kind of international hell that would be stirred up, just to ask you a few questions about Art Rickerby's espionage group?"

"There may have been a revenge angle. I took out a hell of a lot of their people, back in '52."

"Oh, I *remember*..."

She should.

She had been there.

Stark naked, hanging from the rafters by a rope that tore at her wrists as her lovely body twisted slowly in a lantern's light, and the guy in the porkpie had whipped her with a knotted rope, drooling at her in his perverse passion, unaware I was nearby, tommy gun at the ready, and when I let him have it, I made sure the chopper chopped that arm off first so it could drop on the floor in a splash of gore and he could have a goddamn good look at it before I let him have a bellyful of lead.

"Mike—are you all right?" she asked, touching my arm. "I lost you there for a minute."

"I'm fine, kitten. It's just... my little Russian tour stirred some things up."

Her eyes narrowed; they had an almost Asian cast. "You think they went to the trouble of capturing you to even the books for something that happened over ten years ago? That's a long time to wait for revenge."

"Yeah, me, I'm not one of these dish-best-served-cold types. I like it served up hot and right away. But I'm not a Russian. Anyway, there's something much more recent."

Now her eyes widened. "Loose ends from when I was over there?"

"Possibly. And there's the Dragon—I took out the woman and turned the man over to Rickerby, and the K.G.B. was out one top execution team."

*He'd been big, the male half of the Dragon team, a big, big, burly guy
with Apache cheekbones, thick black eyebrows over Slavic-cast eyes, a cruel
slash of a mouth, and we'd fought in that barn to the near death, on top of
each other like rutting beasts only we weren't creating life, we were trying
to end it, his teeth tearing at me, massive fists pounding, butting my head
with his, but in the end I did the smashing and he was a bloody pulp on the
straw-flecked floor as I went looking around until I found a nice big axe that
I was about to bury in his belly until my conscience got the better of me—I
had promised to turn him over alive, to Art Rickerby, who wanted this half
a Dragon to suffer a thousand deaths before three thousand volts finished
the job. To each his own. So I grabbed a twenty-penny nail and a ball-peen
hammer off a workbench and I held the nail in the middle of the back of
his hand and slammed it in with the hammer and slammed and slammed and
slammed until it dimpled the skin, pinning his hand so tight to the wooden
floor he'd never get loose, not without some painful help. Better than handcuffs.
And then I'd called Art.*

Velda had no more questions for me. She had accepted every
word and knew I spoke the truth and that I shared the same
doubts about the Russian motives behind my capture. We had
moved from the couch and I was sipping coffee, with her perched
on the edge of her desk, a frown creasing her eyes.

"What are you going to do, Mike?"

"About what?"

"About what. About being number one on the K.G.B. hit
parade!"

I shrugged. "I go about my business. And wait."

"For how long?"

"Until they make a try. See, it may all be talk. Do they really want to risk blowing this incident up into another missile crisis? What makes me worth that kind of risk?"

She nodded, her lower lip clenched between her teeth. "So that's all you do. Wait and see if they're... all talk."

"No. We're going to work this thing from the New York angle."

"What is there to work?"

"What if Ralph Marley was shot so that I became the guy who accompanied the senator on his Russia trip?"

Her forehead furrowed. "You mean, the K.G.B. wanted to get their hands on you, for whatever reason, and Marley's death paved the way for you to step in?"

"I was the natural second choice for the senator."

"If that's true, that means there *is* a New York angle to this. That there are deep-cover Soviet agents right in this city who manipulated those events."

"Bingo, baby. They are directly responsible for Marley's murder, and they are indirectly responsible for the death of that little Russian doll."

"Did she... mean anything to you, Mike?"

"She was my friend, kitten. She was just a kid who dreamed about defecting and that made her expendable. An enemy of the state. A convenient pawn to be sacrificed in a very crooked game."

"So she *did* mean something to you."

"Whether she did or not, she didn't deserve to die."

Velda swallowed, waved a hand as if using an eraser on blackboard. "No. I'm sorry. I don't mean to sound jealous. Ours is an open relationship. I'm fine about that..."

But was she really? I was the only one taking advantage of that open status. Sometimes I was ashamed of myself. Just never at the right times.

I went over and put my hands on her arms. "Look, if you're right, and there's more to this than just the K.G.B. wanting to grill me about Rickerby's group, or play overdue revenge games on my carcass, then looking into Marley's murder is the place to start. It's the only window into this dark room that we can see into."

"Which means you'll be climbing in through it."

"You got it, sugar."

I didn't have to turn around to know he was there.

That he'd come through that door and was standing behind me—I had felt Velda's body stiffen with a sudden intake of breath and her fingers bite into my upper arm with a spasm of fear.

I turned easily. I was, after all, unarmed.

The squat little guy in the raincoat and gray suit with feathered fedora stood there with one hand in his side pocket, watching us intently. He had the kind of froggy face that split the difference between goofy and sinister. I had seen that expressionless expression on others in the kill racket, and I was wishing I had the .45 that was still locked up in my apartment uptown.

Sloppy, so sloppy. I had dispatched Des Casey to brace this guy, check him out, even take *him out if necessary, and further told the M.P. not to come up to the office right away when he was through with his mission, since I wanted some alone time with Velda. Confidence. Arrogance. A thin line. I'd crossed it. . . .*

Velda's little .22 was on the other side of that desktop where she perched, two and a half feet away. Or was that a million miles?

The froggy face had just started to twist into a peculiar kind of smile when Des Casey came up behind him and laid the leaded end of a collapsible billy over our guest's ear and the feathered fedora took flight while he dropped like all his bones had melted.

"Nice timing, Des," I said. "Velda, Des Casey. Des, Velda Sterling. My partner in crime."

The big sergeant—having traded his M.P. uniform in for a blazer over a gray sweater with white shirt and charcoal slacks—stepped around his fallen victim. He shifted his billy to his left hand so he could shake with Velda, who slid to the floor from the desk perch to smile at our savior.

"You handle that like a pro," Velda said, nodding toward the billy.

"I have a decent batting average," Casey said. He grinned at me. "Now I know why you were so anxious to have some privacy up here. Can't blame you a bit."

Velda gave me a half-smiling look. "So this is the M.P. bodyguard you told me about," she said. "You didn't say he was so good-looking."

She was needling me a little, probably because of that Russian girl, but the way they were measuring each other up had nothing to do with sex—this was two pros recognizing their own kind and enjoying the privilege.

I nodded at the unconscious lump. "Why did it take Froggy so long to come a courting?"

"He made a call in a booth in the lobby," Casey said. "Then he stood around smoking for half an hour until he got called back. Looked like serious conversations."

"And he didn't make you?"

"Naw. I was rapping with the doorman, asking if he had any job leads in the neighborhood." He jerked a thumb at his handiwork on the floor. "What shall we do about our friend?"

"I got him," I said.

I lifted the guy up and threw him on the couch like a bag of laundry. We emptied his pockets and tossed the stuff on the desk. He had a gun all right, but it wasn't in his pocket where his hand had been. It was a .38 Banker's Special in a clip on his belt, and on the other side a leather case held a dozen shells for it. This was my first indication I might have misread the situation—that wasn't the type of rig a hired killer would use at all.

"Oops," Velda said. "Mike, look at this."

She held out our uninvited guest's wallet. Pinned to the inside flap was an agency badge in gold and blue enamel with a matching identity card bearing his photo, prints, and the seal of Rickerby's select group.

Casey, leaning over the guy, gave me an embarrassed glance. "What about it, Mike? Did I screw up?"

"I told Rickerby to lay off. I treat all tails as unfriendly."

"Maybe I hit him too hard…"

"Naw. He's breathing just fine. Get some water, Velda."

She came back in a minute with a glass and I forced him to sip some. His eyes opened gradually, focused on me, and he mumbled, "Jesus Christ…"

Not a prayer.

The welt over his ear looked like a plump sausage. He'd be a long time before putting a hat on again, feathered or otherwise, and a while longer after that before he didn't grimace doing it. He took the glass from my hand, finished its contents, and tried to push himself upright. Velda helped him.

After a few minutes, he was breathing regularly. Finally, he spoke: "That wasn't necessary, Mr. Hammer. Not at all necessary."

I pulled a chair over and sat. "You could have spelled trouble for me, buddy."

His eyes burned holes in my face. "I came here to *identify* myself."

"Why didn't you do it earlier? I spotted you on the plane."

"I was told not to introduce myself until we were in private. Anything in public might mean exposing ourselves unnecessarily. And putting you at risk."

"I told you feds that—"

"I'm *aware* of what you told them," he said curtly.

My hands began to tighten with repressed anger. "Okay. Then I'll tell you again. Any tail on me is going to be treated like the enemy, get it? Sergeant Casey is all the backup I agreed to, and if anybody, however well-meaning, adds to that, and winds up hurt? It's their own damn fault."

His smile intermingled indignation and discomfort. "I will be sure to underscore that in my report." He touched the side of his head gingerly, and winced. "Now, since you've destroyed my usefulness, at least temporarily, I'll get back to the office. If you don't mind." He paused, then said: "You'll stay in touch, of course."

"I told your boss I would."

"I know. And he told me to remind you to do so." The froggy little man sighed, then lurched to his feet. "May I have my things?"

"Not a problem," I said, and I went and got his gun, glancing at the I.D. in his wallet before handing the stuff over, saying,

"Friendly word of advice, Mr. Rath. Stay the hell out of my hair."

"Don't worry about that, Mr. Hammer. Once I report in, I'll be assigned to a desk for a while, and glad to be." He grunted some displeasure, then put his gun in the hip holster, and the wallet in his pocket, gave us one last disgusted look, and went out the door.

"Your friend Rickerby didn't waste any time," Casey said.

"I didn't expect him to," I said.

"Think we'll get any hassle over that?"

"Nope. I told Art what to expect, and I'm sure he passed that on down along the line."

Casey laughed without much humor. "Too bad nobody told *that* poor slob."

"*Mike…*"

I turned and Velda was sitting in her desk chair, holding the drinking glass up to the light.

"What?"

"Come here." Her tone was no-nonsense.

I walked over. "You have something?"

"Take a look at this." Wearing a nasty little smile, Velda rolled the glass around in the overhead light until it caught a clear print on the side. "That's his. Our guest's."

"That could be my print or yours, baby. But so what if it's his?"

She put the glass down carefully and her eyes were intense. "I just cleaned those glasses. No one else used that."

"So?"

"So when you threw that's guy's wallet over here, I checked his I.D. Photo looked like him, all right, or enough so that I didn't pay much attention. What I did happen to notice, just by dumb luck, was his thumb print. The central pattern was a distinct whorl with a scar through it." She nodded toward the displayed print in the light. "The right thumb print on the glass is a loop. No scar."

I felt the chill go right through me. "Damn!"

Casey, yanking a .38 Special from under his left arm, was already out the door, checking the hallway.

Velda said, "Better make a call, Mike."

I reached for her phone, direct-dialed the D.C. number I'd long since committed to memory, and got Art Rickerby on the line. When he answered I said, "Mike Hammer, Art."

"You must be back in the city by now. What is it, Mike?"

"You have an agent named Herman Rath?"

There was a silence of maybe three seconds before Rickerby said, "What do you know about him?"

There was a tight, cold edge to his voice.

"Let's have it, Art."

"Rath committed suicide here in Washington about an hour before you left. He was on an extended leave having to do with health problems. There was no connection to—"

"His gun belt and wallet were missing. Right?"

"…Where are you, Mike?"

"My office in Manhattan."

"Then you just stay put until my people can get there."

"You're already too late, buddy. He's out the door."

"You just *stay* there."

"I'm not going anywhere."

I hung up.

Casey came back in, tucking away the .38. He shook his head.

"Checked the stairs, the restrooms. He's in the wind, Mike."

Velda and Casey faced me, their arms folded, waiting to hear how I read it.

"It might have been a hit attempt," I said, "but what I think they were doing was testing our defenses. If we had been sloppy enough, and we damn near were, it might have gone down right here and now. But this feels like recon—now they know about you, Des. And they know you're my only backup. *Why* do they know? Because, goddamnit, I *told* them."

I slammed a fist on the desk and Velda's roses jumped.

"Maybe we should close down the office for a while," Velda said. She turned to Casey. "We have a string of apartments and small hotels available as safe houses for witnesses. Just like the cops. We can bounce from one to the other, till this is over."

I said, "No way, doll. They don't scare me out of my own damn Batcave. Anyway, they'll try it a different way, next time."

Casey's voice was a low growl. "Who *was* he, Mike?"

"The first of many," I said.

It was midnight before they got through with us. A retired police artist was called in to sketch a picture of the suspect from our description until we were satisfied it could be used for identification. A photo of the late Herman Rath revealed a general physical resemblance that a quick look would buy, but that might not have stood up to a closer inspection.

Des Casey was able to provide the license number of the cab the fake Rath used. That meant the cabbie could be shown the police sketch for verification, and the same would be true for the flight crew on the shuttle plane from D.C.

Apparently Herman Rath had been selected because he had the same basic physical characteristics as the enemy agent who tailed us or possibly vice versa. Rath died in his own apartment in what was now believed to be a murder staged as a suicide. His body had not been not found for several hours, and the missing gun and wallet had not been initially noticed.

The sophistication of seeking a near lookalike among federal agents for the substitution of their own agent could mean only one thing. The Soviets were expending all of their resources on this effort. We weren't up against one assassin or even a team or two of them—we had an entire espionage organization opposing us.

The print on the glass was obviously not Rath's. It was classified by an expert on the spot, then rushed to the local office of Rickerby's group for Telexing to Washington, where it was run through their computerized files without a match. A copy was fired off to several foreign police bureaus, but nobody seemed hopeful that anything would come of it.

From my desk, I spoke on the phone with Rickerby while his men were still there taking Velda's statement.

"Mike, this is going to increase the heat I'll be getting from inside my agency and without. They'll be after me again to keep you under wraps."

"Remind them I have legal rights and will fight them down the line. If they want that kind of news coverage, they can go for it. You do know I number Hy Gardner among my best buddies?"

"Well, Hy Gardner and *no* reporter can have this story, Mike,"

Rickerby said, insistent. "This is strictly classified. The real Herman Rath stays a suicide, and nobody came around your office this afternoon except maybe the cleaning lady."

"If so, she looked like a frog and packed a pistol."

"You surely realize this means that we have to give you more protection than just Sergeant Casey."

"Hell you say. You're gonna lay a cover on me *now*?"

"My agent-in-charge there will fill you in," Rickerby said, and hung up. Not so much as a goodbye. What did I ever do to deserve such rude treatment?

"Don't worry, Mr. Hammer," a tall blond agent in his early thirties told me. He had the kind of blandly handsome face that didn't look like it had had much use. "We'll be discreet about it."

"Is that right?"

"We'll have two men in an apartment across the street from yours, and an office down the hall here at the Hackard Building has already been rented to one of our dummy corporations. And a pair of female agents will be down the hall from Miss Sterling's apartment, keeping watch."

"Son, this is a crafty, canny bunch we're up against with a real grasp of spy craft. I'll lay you odds our K.G.B. pals will take note of those new rentals."

"We're not naive, Mr. Hammer, nor are we inexperienced. It may interest you to know we anticipated your actions before you ever got back. Those places were rented then."

"Okay. So your boss knows his stuff."

Still, he didn't appreciate the doubts I'd expressed at all. "We'll keep a nominal check on your activities, Mr. Hammer.

We won't be in your way. The personnel we assign will be highly experienced."

"They'd better be. I haven't seen a federal tail yet that I couldn't shake if I felt like it."

His face settled into a cold mask. "Perhaps you don't realize the gravity of your situation, Hammer."

No "mister" now.

"Ever kill a man?" I asked him.

His head went back, as if I had slapped him.

"Men somewhere out in that city," I said, with a nod toward the window on the nighttime world that was Manhattan, "are preparing to kill me. And if you think I don't understand the gravity of that 'situation,' check my record, and see how many have tried… and died."

He had no reply. He just gave me a steady stare for a few seconds, then gathered his team and left. I was still seated at my desk. The spot in my thigh where I'd taken that bullet for Marley felt like a small misplaced toothache, a nagging little reminder of how this whole vicious mess began.

A while back, Velda and I had taken apartments in the same building—it came in handy for business conferences and the like. Also, remind me to sell you the Brooklyn Bridge. I sent Casey on ahead with the key to mine, then walked Velda up to hers.

She invited me in, but I said, "We'll have a real reunion when this settles down," and she gave me a long, lingering kiss that was a dare to do otherwise, then smiled devilishly, said, "Your loss," and shut me out in the hall.

I went back up to my pad, 9-D, where Casey was waiting just

inside, with the door open. While it was pretty much as I'd left it, the telltale signs were there.

"A nice, thorough, professional job," Casey said.

"Guess you can't say the place was tossed," I said, "when they're this careful."

Locked drawers had been neatly opened and closed without forcing them, but scraps of paper I'd inserted to betray tampering were gone. So was the single hair stretched across the concealed gun cabinet built into the closet wall. None of the firearms appeared messed with, though.

The big tell was a funny one—the apartment had been closed up for over two months, but there wasn't any dust. They'd had to clean up after themselves because otherwise the dust would have betrayed them.

Casey asked, "Anything missing?"

"Not that I can see without a full-scale inventory."

"Were they looking for something?"

"Don't know. Just poking around, I think. Getting to know their prey."

I went to the window on the street. The building across the way had been renovated and refaced while I was away. Most of the windows were slatted with Venetian blinds and it was impossible to tell which apartment belonged to Rickerby's boys.

Casey said, "So how does it feel, being a piece of cheese that's waiting for a rat to take a bite?"

"It stinks, friend. But there are lots of ways to deal with rats."

I went over and pulled the .45 out of the wall cabinet, shoved a full clip into the end of the butt, jacked a shell into the chamber, and thumbed the hammer on half-cock, then to safety. My hand felt complete.

I hefted the weapon. "You tell me, Des, how the hell are they're gonna stop me?"

"Simple. Manpower."

I grinned at him. "Ever hear of Charlie One-Horse?"

Casey shook his head.

But I didn't explain.

We got Blue Ribbons from the fridge and wound up in my little TV room with Johnny Carson going. We were both in athletic T-shirts and trousers, and the Negro's massive musculature bore the puckered indentations and white scars that lived under that chestful of ribbons.

"Okay," the M.P. said. "I'll bite at the cheese. Who was Charlie One-Horse?"

"An Indian who declared a one-man war against the U.S. Army back in the eighteen-seventies. He did millions of dollars worth of damage to government property, knocked off a few hundred soldiers, and kept several regiments detached from regular duty just to catch him."

"Did they ever?"

"Yeah, but not because the Army was that good. Charlie's wife was having a baby and he wasn't willing to leave her by herself just so he could get away again."

"What happened? Firing squad?"

"You kidding? They handled him with kid gloves and tenderly put him down in nice quarters on his own reservation. They were afraid there might be more like him, out in the hills and valleys and plains, and they couldn't afford the action."

"So now you're Charlie One-Horse, I suppose?"

"Let's just say I'm on the war path. You keep watching Carson, buddy." I hauled myself to my feet. "Charlie One-Horse need shuteye."

Then I was climbing between clean, crisp sheets. Nice to be back in my own rack again.

With that .45 under the spare pillow where it belonged.

CHAPTER SEVEN

The law offices of Carmichael, Jasper and Porter were located in the Breck-Stillwell Building in midtown Manhattan, another of those imposing new structures defacing the city like steel-and-glass tombstones erected to the death of individuality.

Although Allen Jasper still was a partner, he took no active role in the firm while he held his seat in the Senate, chiefly using his office to conduct government business when he was away from D.C.

Des Casey and I entered a lushly wood-paneled waiting room about the size of the suite Allen and I had shared back at the Hotel National in Moscow. Each of the law partners had his own secretary at a desk. I directed Casey to a comfortable-looking couch, where he selected a *Life* magazine from an end table—the place was so high rent, the magazines were current issues.

Senator Jasper's secretary had been with him forever, a prim little old lady type who still wore lace at her throat.

She expressed her disapproval of me by peering over her silver-framed slanting bifocals and pretending she didn't know me. But she knew me, all right. Brother, how she knew me.

She asked my name.

"Paul Revere," I said.

"Do you have an appointment?"

"No. Just tell Allen the Redcoats are coming."

She reached for the intercom to announce me, but I didn't wait and smiled at the indignant squawk I heard behind me as I walked on into his big private office.

This was a chamber as almost as large as the waiting room, with the same rich masculine walls, the one at left arrayed with photographs of the senator with celebrities ranging from other political figures to supporters among the Hollywood crowd. The dominant picture, however, was a large elaborately framed family portrait, taken perhaps ten years ago, of Allen, his wife Emily, and their children.

His work area was to the right as you entered, given over to some wooden file cabinets and a mahogany desk no bigger than a Sherman tank, its top neatly arranged with stacks of paperwork. But straight ahead, across the expanse of wall-to-wall rust-color carpeting, next to a postcard-worthy window on Manhattan, was an area for entertaining visitors, with modern-styled but comfortable-looking chairs and a couch. A wet bar, which could be concealed by a built-in folding screen, was showing off enough fancy bottles of booze to satisfy a Stork Club bartender.

Senator Allen Jasper, his rangy frame in a sharply tailored suit, was just coming around that bar with a cocktail in either hand. It was only mid-morning, but hell, it must have been five o'clock somewhere. Who could blame him? He was in the company of a beautiful woman.

His lovely guest's cocktail dress further justified letting that wet bar breathe. Her high-necked dress was a shimmering money-green that draped a full-figured body that spelled out total sexual maturity. Nature had been considerate to this woman once upon a time and she had spent the years since not taking that for granted.

What nature had endowed, she had nurtured so that any man seeing this woman felt as if he had an engraved invitation in his hand... addressed to somebody else. Her hair seemed to be platinum at first, but on closer inspection I made it a premature white, yet still possessing the silky softness of youth.

Jasper didn't hear me come in. He was busy setting the drink before her on the glass coffee table near the couch. They were talking and joking, her laughter with a high-pitched tinkly quality to it that even the senator's booming voice couldn't conquer.

I called out, "Hope I'm not interrupting anything, Senator."

Recognizing the voice, he glanced my way with an immediate smile and came across the room with those long bird-legged strides. He grabbed my hand as if saving somebody falling off a building.

"Mike, damn it man, I've been waiting for you to get in touch! Man, am I glad to see you, alive and well."

I grinned at him; he was still pumping my hand. "Yeah, well, it was touch and go for a while."

His expression turned serious, almost somber, and there was embarrassment in it. "I'm surprised you're even speaking to me."

"Why, Allen?"

"I wouldn't be surprised if you thought I'd hung you out to dry, when I wasn't there at the Pentagon to back you up. But I couldn't get in to be part of that. So much for senatorial privilege!"

"You didn't miss anything much."

"That alphabet soup of agencies put on a hell of an act in Washington to sidetrack me when you got back. I finally just said to hell with it. I knew those bureaucrats wouldn't be any match for you, Mike."

"I figured it was something like that."

He took me by the arm and ushered me deeper into the office. "I want you to meet somebody." He walked me over to the stunning older woman. He grinned at her the way a father does when he's giving his spoiled little girl a pony. "Irene… this is Mike Hammer. Mike, Irene Carroll."

"Hello, Mike," she said, standing. "If I may take that liberty?"

"Take all the liberties you like," I said.

She held out her hand and I accepted it like a reward. She had a soft, warm grip, but there was strength there too. "I've heard so much about you, it's hard to believe you're real."

"If not, I've done a good job fooling myself," I said.

"In fact," she said, leaning toward me confidentially, "I rather intruded on Allen so that I could meet you."

"Then you must be psychic," I said, lightly, "since Allen didn't know I was stopping by."

Jasper said, "Oh, I told Irene I figured I'd be hearing from you this morning. You recognize the name, of course?"

I nodded. Hell, who didn't know Irene Carroll? You could sum her up by newspaper shorthand: Wealthy Widow, Prominent Socialite, Washington Hostess. Intimate of kings and presidents and (when necessary) dictators. Tosser of the biggest parties in Washington and provider of the terrain for the policy-makers of the world to maneuver on.

The celebrated Washington hostess notorious for wearing a queen's fortune of jewels to her own and the parties of others… *who had been absent from the senator's shindig the night the shooting had started.*

"Judging by the press coverage," she said with the kind of perfect smile that requires practice, "they haven't decided yet whether you're a national hero or an international heel."

I gave her my own grin, which had required no practice at all. "I bet you remember what Rhett Butler told Scarlett O'Hara just before the fadeout."

That made her laugh some more, that many-faceted laugh with more tones than a wind chime.

Allen Jasper threw his arm around my shoulder. "Well, even if you *don't* give a damn, Mike, I'm going to do everything in my power to see to it personally that the public gets the real facts."

When you'd been in Washington as long as Jasper, you had to differentiate between the real facts and the other kind.

I gave him a choppy laugh. "Allen, will you quit talking like a politician? What the public thinks matters to me not a whit. What I don't go for is being the brunt of extradition efforts. Look at that legally and see what comes up."

Jasper nodded, his eyes narrowing shrewdly. A lot of people thought him just a politico when he had one of the best legal minds in New York.

"I'll do that, my friend," he assured me.

Irene Carroll put her drink down and her light manner disappeared. "Could I be of any help, Mike?"

"Why?"

The short question caught her off guard, but she recovered fast. "If you're Allen's friend, you're my friend. I move in powerful circles, Mike. Affairs of this nature aren't new to me."

"Ever been shot at, Irene?"

Her eyes crinkled. "Well… hardly."

"Then it's new to you."

She thought about whether to be offended, then—to her credit—that tinkly laugh blossomed again and pleasure showed in her expression. "You know, Mike, meeting you is even more fun than hearing about all your *wild* adventures."

"Meaning no offense, Irene, to me they aren't adventures. They're a matter of life and death."

She raised a conciliatory palm. "I mean no offense, either. But it was worth the trip from Washington just to hear a man talk who doesn't monitor his every word. If I ever *do* get shot, I'll be sure to come to you for advice about what to do about it."

"Check in with a doctor first," I said with a smile, "but after that, I'll be glad to consult."

She reached for the mink stole slung over the back of a nearby chair. Speaking archly, she said, "I know you boys have a lot to talk about that an innocent girl shouldn't hear… so I'll say *ciao*."

But she took my hand again, and gave me an impish wink. Her voice took on a kittenish purr that had also taken practice. "Why don't you call me, Mike? I'd like to pick up our conversation where it left off."

"You still at the Wentworth?" I asked.

"Yes. It's a *real* invitation, Mike. I'm not just being polite."

"You'll hear from me, Irene," I said.

"I'll look forward to it." Almost as an afterthought, she turned to her host and said, "Goodbye, Allen. Please give my best to Emily."

"I'll be sure to," he said. "Thanks for stopping by."

The way she swept out, you would think she'd brought a retinue with her.

"Now there's a broad," I said.

Jasper chuckled. "Yes, and I'm sure she'd take no offense at having Mike Hammer call her one. They just don't make 'em like that anymore."

Maybe. But when you did make them, you could have a real good time....

The senator was heading over to the wet bar, where he'd left his drink. "You want anything, Mike?"

"Little early."

"Mine's just a Coke. You want one?"

"Sure."

While he fixed me up, I took a walk around the spacious chamber. It didn't take me long to spot the miniature microphone built right into one of the artificial flowers that decorated a cabinet along one wall.

Astonished, he watched me pluck it out, trace the lead inside the cabinet to a transistorized voice-activated recorder. He started to speak, and I raised a hand.

I knew what he didn't: that the pros plant decoys. I found the real ones under the window sills by the little living room area and also behind his desk. I ripped both loose. I pronounced the office debugged, and then we were sitting across from each other in comfy chairs, the coffee table between us with Irene's drink still on it, a reminder of her recent company.

Jasper was studying me with a touch of amazement mingled with anger. "Just like Moscow," he said. "How did you know they'd be there?"

"Because they're covering all the angles."

"By 'they' do you mean our side or theirs?"

"Our people know better." Anyway, Art Rickerby did. He'd know I'd check for electronic eavesdropping before saying anything worth hearing. "This is our K.G.B. pals."

"You're only back a day!"

"Allen, they're way ahead of us. They *knew* I'd be coming here, if I made it home, and they had these things installed long ago."

"The K.G.B.... here in Manhattan? How—"

I cut him short. "Money can buy almost anything, buddy. A window washer, maybe somebody posing as the building janitor, a phone company rep... anybody. Check with your secretary. She'll know who had access to your office in the last few weeks."

His eyes were narrow slits now. "They'll have to come back for them, won't they? To check and find what they got?"

"They'll be monitoring their recorders from a remote location. You think we can search every room in this building? And if I put the feds on that job, the other side'll know we're on to them, and just leave the electronic toys behind."

"But if we *don't* let on that we're on to them, at some point those toys will be retrieved, right?"

"Forget it, Allen. You'll nail some joker who never knew the score in the first place. Frankly, I think it's another test."

I gave him a rundown on my caller at the office yesterday, and watched him tighten up like a tick about to burst.

"Damn it, Mike, this has gone beyond the jurisdiction of any of these federal investigative agencies. This requires congressional action!"

"Spare me, Allen. Like anything ever comes of those hearings."

He flinched. That one had hurt.

I waved dismissively. "If I had been knocked off yesterday, everything would be settled by now. To the Kremlin crowd, as long as I'm breathing, I'm a major embarrassment. But what I want to settle is why I got snatched off that Moscow street."

"Don't we know that already? Weren't you grabbed for the propaganda value, and to get back at you for past 'sins against the State'?"

"Then why didn't they grab me the minute I set foot on Russian soil?"

"I can answer that, Mike. That would have *guaranteed* an international incident. They had okayed your entry into the country as my approved bodyguard, and arresting you would have been obvious trickery. Instead, they set up that business about you passing off money to a known dissident."

My fists tightened. "Our innocent little translator."

His face fell. "Poor Zora. She was their dupe in this travesty, this tragedy."

"So were we. But that justified my arrest."

He nodded. "Right. They had allowed you in as my bodyguard, in good faith, but you 'betrayed' that trust by engaging in espionage activities."

I sipped my Coke. "What happened on your end, after they dragged me off?"

Jasper laughed again, humorlessly this time. "I became *persona non grata* immediately. I was ushered out like a drunken bum being thrown out of a saloon."

"Immediately?"

"Damn near. When I heard of your arrest, I lodged a protest with the American embassy. I was on the phone with our people when an M.V.D. contingent arrived to escort me to the airport, where I was put aboard an Aeroflot plane bound for the States. By then, you had broken loose and there wasn't anything more to do but wait. I've been catching a lot of political hell since."

"I can imagine."

"I'm not sure you can, Mike. Luckily, your escapade over there played like something out of Hitchcock. I was lost in the first reel, and you became the hero or villain, depending on the audience's political point of view. In a way, you took the curse off me. You always were good news copy anyway, and this latest episode…"

He let the sentence hang there because my expression had turned into a scowl.

"They were going to kill me, Allen."

"I didn't mean to sound like I took it lightly, Mike."

I leaned back and rubbed my aching thigh. "If you had used Marley as your bodyguard, none of this would have happened. How did you come to choose me as his substitute?"

The bluntness of that made him flinch. "Are you asking me as a friend, Mike? Or suspect?"

"Let's keep it friendly."

"I've seen that look on your face before. You aren't quite sure about me, are you?"

"Does it matter?"

"But you'll check me out, is that it?"

"All the way, Senator. I'm setting the machinery in motion today."

"Then let me anticipate the result. I've never lied to you, Mike."

"Have you held back any aspect of how I came to replace Ralph Marley?"

"No. Nothing."

"The job you hired me for... Marley's job... what I know it to be is the extent of it?"

"Absolutely."

"And no one suggested to you that I be chosen as Marley's replacement?"

"No one." He shifted on the chair, sighed, gestured with an open hand. "Marley I knew for a long time. Used his services on numerous occasions. His job was exactly the same one you took over. Since he was an employee of the agency I hired him through, he must have filed reports that you should be able to get access to. I would appreciate it if you checked into the matter thoroughly."

"I intend to," I said.

He gave me a sad, wry smile. "After what we've been through together, I'm sorry it's necessary at all."

Actually we hadn't been through that much together, just the preliminary part of my Russian "adventure," as Irene Worth had put it.

"No one pressured you to take me along," I said, trying again.

"No." He shrugged. "You were there that night when Marley was shot. You were the hero of the hour. You were the logical, natural choice. There was nothing sinister about it, Mike. All right?"

"All right," I said. "I'm glad we cleared the air."

His smile turned sideways and he shook his head. "You're a tough man, Mike."

"I have to be," I said.

At the Blue Ribbon Restaurant on West Forty-fourth Street, I positioned Des Casey at the bar and went to my regular table in the corner where two walls of autographed celebrity pictures looked over your shoulder while you ate. Velda came gliding in, getting her usual round of amazed silent wolf whistles and wide-eyed stares of male approval. Women were divided on the subject of Velda: some could appreciate what God collaborating with a beautiful woman could accomplish, and the rest flat-out hated her.

She wore a navy-blue tailored suit that but for a near-mini-length skirt couldn't have been more conservative and yet didn't hide a single curve. Those crazy long legs of hers were a stimulant more potent than any double martini the bar could serve up.

When she sat down, I said, "They're looking at you like you should be on the menu."

She shot me that funny little smile and her eyes crinkled with warmth. "At ease, you."

"I'm not at attention yet."

"Give it time." She passed me a manila folder thick with onionskin second sheets of original reports. "The New York branch of Ralph Marley's California office was glad to cooperate."

"They had these on file?"

"Because Marley was killed in New York, these papers were transferred in case the NYPD needed them."

"But of course they didn't."

Velda nodded. "Too open-and-shut."

"Why is it the open-and-shut cases so often need re-opening? It's a rhetorical question. Brief me."

She signaled for a drink, then leaned forward on the table, the dark arcs of the page boy swinging nicely. "Those are Marley's daily reports to the office on every occasion when he was assigned to the senator."

"Good."

"Not really. Every bit of it is routine. All simple watchdog work. No special instructions. There were a few predictable incidents, given Jasper's conservative leanings… fanatics trying to break up a speech, threatening letters and the like, but nothing really unusual."

"Okay."

"I called Mercer, the head man in the California office, and he said Marley was pretty bored with working for the senator. That he didn't especially enjoy the assignment, but that the senator thought a lot of Marley and requested his services each time."

"Any tie-ins with other jobs?"

"Nothing, Mike. All of Marley's other assignments in the same period were in the industrial field—checking out inventory losses, guarding payrolls, that sort of standard stuff. Nothing he did ever brought him into in contact with any of the senator's associates, at least that we know of."

"He ever say why he didn't want to work for Jasper anymore?"

Velda nodded. "Boredom. Nothing personal—apparently he thought the senator was an all right guy. Marley just liked the industrial end better, and staying home in California. He was married, you know, with three kids. Very conservative himself, in the lifestyle sense, anyway."

"Yeah, I know. Ralph had an eye for the ladies but he never did anything about it that I know of. A real family man. Loved his wife exclusively."

"A dying breed, I hear," she said, giving me a look.

"Skip the comedy. What else?"

"Mercer admitted he was irritated with Ralph, because they might lose the gig. The senator was partial to having Ralph around."

"And Mercer wasn't anxious to lose such a high-paying client."

She was nodding. "Which is why Marley stayed on the job. He suffered through it. I got the impression that he couldn't stand either political party, and the general D.C. crowd the senator was associated with."

"Yeah," I grunted, "I can imagine."

I thumbed through the sheets in the folder and pulled out the last one. It was the final report Marley had submitted, the day before he was killed. In addition to a summary of the day's activities, it included a proposed program for the following day, concluding with the party at the senator's apartment and the guest list. I took down the names and addresses in my little notebook, stuffed the rest back in the folder, and handed it back to Velda.

"Get copies made and return these," I told her.

"Will do." She pointed to the names in my notebook, which I was studying. "Shall I follow up on those?"

I tore the page out and then in half and gave her the lower section. "Take these. I'll check the rest out."

She glanced over the sheet and frowned. "You can get most of their histories in the public library, you know. If you're looking for suspects, these are primarily public figures."

"So was John Wilkes Booth," I said.

"You know that bothering these people will raise all kinds of hell, don't you? And you have enough pressure on you, already."

"Not if you do it right," I said with a shrug. "Call Hy Gardner and our other columnist friends. See what the names on that list have to hide."

"Who says they do?"

"Doll, I never saw anybody that didn't have something to hide. Find out first what that is, and they'll cooperate, all right."

"You're a bastard, Mike," she said, grinning, shaking her head, the black hair shimmering.

"Don't try to sell that tip to the columnists," I said, grinning back at her. "That's very old news."

We had some lunch.

She was gathering her purse to go, when she said, "You want me to dump those shadows the Feds have on me?"

I shook my head. "No, they aren't interested in interfering with your business. They're just concerned with you staying healthy and in circulation."

"Why are they interested in *my* welfare all of a sudden?"

"Because you can be used as a lever against me. It's been done enough times in the past."

A look of extreme concern clenched her pretty face. "Mike— why is the K.G.B. risking blowing up a minor international incident into a major one, just to take *you* out? They haven't lost *that* much face... have they?"

"I'll be damned if I know, doll, but I've never been an expert on Soviet thinking." We got up and were heading out. Des Casey fell in behind us. "I'll check with you at your apartment tonight, doll."

"You better."

"After all these months without you, how could I not?"

Her teeth showed in a wicked smile between lush lips that promised more than a man should know about in advance, her eyes a brown velvet fire.

"Thinking about catching up, are you?" she said.

"Get out of here," I said. "Get to work!"

She was going to kill me before the K.G.B. did.

But what a way to go.

Des Casey didn't like what I was asking of him.

"Sticking with you, man," he said, "that's my job. I can just picture my stripes going down the crapper after you get picked off, and me not around to pick up the pieces."

I put my hand on my heart. "And wasn't that a touching speech?"

We were standing out in front of the Blue Ribbon. Ricochets of sunlight were bouncing off buildings but the afternoon was chilly, the fall weather just starting to assert itself.

I didn't have to be told that my personal M.P. had special orders to make regular reports to Art Rickerby, with the agents shadowing us at a distance sure to report that he'd split off from me.

We climbed in back of a cab together.

"Look, Mike," Casey said apologetically, "I know you can brush me anytime you feel like it. So I'm gonna do what you ask. You just cover me the best you can."

"Don't kid a kidder, Des. It's not a reprimand you're afraid of. You're just worried you're going to miss some of the action."

He didn't deny it, but did return my grin.

The M.P. already had his assignment—I wanted him to run a check on Allen Jasper, and jotted some names and numbers on a notebook page of resources whose reliability was well-tested, from longtime snitches to Hy Gardner and his newspaperman peers. Casey let out a low whistle when he saw some of the latter names, but didn't question it any. I had already arranged for the Blue Ribbon to serve as our contact point, with George, the owner, and his wife Angie—both old friends—handling the communications.

We shared a cab for a short trip downtown and went through a regular procedure I had used before to shake anybody on my tail. It was a routine I had set up a long time ago, which included two quick wrong-way trips down one-way streets, and cost a ten spot every time I used it.

When I was certain we were clear, I said so long to Casey, let him keep the ride, and climbed out to flag down the next cruising cab, where I settled back in the cushions. That ache in my thigh was still acting up, a heavy muscle wound with some bite to remind me I wasn't getting any younger. I closed my eyes until we reached the dusty brick building out of which worked Captain Pat Chambers of the Homicide Division.

I stood in the doorway of Pat's office until he looked up, then grinned at him slowly. There had been times when we were friends and times when we were enemies. We knew each other so well each could anticipate the other's every word and action. Right now we were friends again, a pair of old pros whose jobs sent us both into New York's jungle of violent crime, a jungle that with each passing year seemed to grow ever more dense and thick, inhabited by ever more dangerous predators.

Even after more than two months, there was no hello, no handshake. He just looked up at me like a teacher who had caught a pupil clowning in front of the class.

His mouth managed not to smile but those gray-blue eyes did it anyway. "Where do you get your luck, Mike?"

"What do you care?" I said. "It's all bad."

"Well, you're still walking around," he said.

"That's not luck, Pat." I tossed my hat on his desk and sat down. "That's survival instinct."

He shoved some paperwork away and closed the folder he had been studying. "I heard about a few of your detractors who *didn't* survive... About forty-five of them?"

"Ah. You've been reading my publicity."

He leaned back in his swivel chair. "Read it! Hell, I helped write it. Washington picked up on every file with your name in it in the NYPD system, and had me type out a twenty-page report on my personal association with you."

"I hope you made me look good."

"Let's just say I didn't make any fans upstairs."

"You'll never make inspector that way."

"Not helping you, I won't."

"We closed a lot of cases, buddy."

"But damn few made it into the courts. They all seem to end with somebody dead."

"As long it's not me or you, what's the problem?"

A trace of a smile showed at one corner of his mouth. "Funny thing. I think the Justice Department boys were a little shook at the people who came to your defense. You have some powerful friends in some strange places. What have you got on them, Mike?"

"Just favors owed," I said.

"Like that guy Rickerby, huh? And what favor do you want from me?"

I leaned forward just a little. "When the G came sniffing around about me, did they make any inquiries about the night I was in that shoot-out at Jasper's penthouse pad?"

"Just that they wanted to know how you happened to be hired for that particular job."

"What did you tell them, Pat?"

"That Marley asked you to give him a hand. That you and he had a history of sending work each other's way. And that Senator Jasper approved Marley's request. That was all in my report. You still haven't asked me for the favor yet."

"What can you tell me about the guy who killed Marley?"

"And wounded the great Mike Hammer, who promptly sent him on a twelve-story swan dive?" Pat shrugged. "Pietro Romanos, smalltime local hood with nine arrests and two convictions. Don't you remember, Mike? We went over this at the time."

"Not in detail. What did Romanos go down for?"

Another shrug. "Robbery the first time, aggravated assault the second. He did short time that didn't seem to teach him a lesson. He was reputedly the bagman for Harris before Harris got killed in Newark. As far as we know, he was working the stolen car racket after that."

"And you figure the motive at the senator's party was robbery?"

"There was a lot of ice being worn that night. You know the Carroll woman?"

"I met her earlier today," I said.

"You'll recall that she was late to the party—showed up after you got hit and were carted off to get patched up. Rolled in wearing her usual quarter million in gems."

"How would Romanos have known she'd be there?"

"That we don't know."

"Okay, so somehow he knew she'd be there. How did he know she'd be wearing the jewels?"

"Hell, Mike, that broad never shows up at a party without the damn things. She's so careless about it she can't get them insured."

"Well, with her kind of loot, Pat, she can just buy more. Like when you run out of toilet paper."

"Maybe so, but that ice makes pretty good bait for a punk like that Romanos." He shook his head, chuckled. "You know, you don't know how lucky you were."

"So you still think I'm lucky?"

"Damn straight. That little hood had a reputation we knew

nothing about. He was a firearms buff. When we shook down his pad, we came up with twelve pieces in top working order and six hundred rounds of assorted ammunition. Eight of those pieces were target pistols of various calibers, and his prized possessions were trophies he picked up at matches around the country. Seems like he worked the state fairs and gave exhibitions at any given opportunity."

"So when he went up against me, he went up against somebody better."

"Taking nothing away from your modesty, pal, I doubt it. He went there to knock the place off, expecting to find one man on duty, ran into two. He took care of Marley, didn't he?"

I mulled it. "Maybe he wasn't there for a heist at all, Pat. A guy with his firearms skills has the makings of an assassin. He was heading right for Senator Jasper when Marley jumped in front of the bullet."

Pat said nothing for a few moments. Then he said, "I could maybe buy that. The senator is a controversial figure. There are plenty who would like to see him silenced, and uh… there is *one* thing we turned up that might help substantiate your theory."

"Share the wealth, Pat."

"Well, it struck me as peculiar at the time. Just two weeks before the shooting at Jasper's place, Romanos deposited one hundred grand in a savings account."

"A pay-off. For a political assassination?"

He shook his head. "That's not my bailiwick, man. Not my area of expertise."

"Was it the 'bailiwick' of those feds you made the report to?"

He nodded. "I passed that info on. But obviously, Romanos himself is a literal dead-end."

"And isn't that convenient."

"Well, you shot him." He frowned. "You think it was a political hit, and Jasper ducked a bullet with his name on it?"

I shrugged. "All I know for sure, Pat, is that it all started that night. And *I* was supposed to be dead by now, too."

Pat locked his fingers behind his head and leaned back in his chair. "Maybe it's time you told me about your summer vacation."

I took a half hour to spell it all out to him and watched him put the pieces of information into mental slots where he could analyze them later. The computer between that guy's ears was something IBM would love to invent.

When I finished, he tilted forward and tapped a pencil against his desk. "So Senator Jasper was an assassination target?"

"Probably," I said, "but a lot of prominent people were there that night. No matter who the victim, if Romanos was on a contract kill, then somebody was paying for it."

For a while Pat was silent, then he looked up, his eyes tight. "That's a pretty cold trail by now. Unless the feds are pursuing it."

I stood up. "Will you look into it?"

"I'll have to make the suggestion upstairs. Washington is laying down some pretty heavy flak."

"Screw them. Ralph Marley is a homicide, and the last time I looked you were *Captain* of Homicide. And this homicide went down in *your* jurisdiction. Or is that 'bailiwick?'"

He let the grin crack through his frown. "You never change, do you? Okay, I'll push the issue. We'll backtrack on Romanos and see where it leads. But, listen, Mike…"

"Yeah, yeah," I said, holding my hands up in surrender, "I know, I know. If I come up with anything, call you first."

He wagged a finger at me. "You obstruct justice, pal, and I'll throw your ass in the slammer as fast as the next bad guy's."

"You never change either," I said, on my way out. "Do you, Pat?"

CHAPTER EIGHT

New York had clouded up again and the musky smell of rain was in the air. I stood in the doorway of Pat's precinct building and cased the street, watching the traffic carefully. A row of police cruisers stood at the curb and the flow moved by cautiously. A few other cars were parked farther down and the taxi I'd arrived in sat in a slot outside a coffee house. I'd paid the cabbie twenty to sit with his meter off and his top light unlit while I was in with Pat, so I'd be assured of a fast exit.

There are times when you can feel the trouble hovering, waiting to drop right on top of you. Even though I couldn't put my finger on it, I knew it was there. The police aren't the only ones who can sift through a person's background and come up with information like known associates. Anybody who took even a casual stroll through my history would learn just how often Pat and I had worked together, and could stake out this building—even if it was a police station—to see if I'd show.

Inside the station house's high-ceilinged reception area, where a desk sergeant ruled from on high, I wedged into a pay booth, not needing anybody's permission for my one phone call. I thumbed through the directory until I found the number of the nearby coffee house and got the manager to send a waitress out to summon my cabbie to the phone.

"This is your fare," I said.

"That twenty bucks won't last forever, bud."

"My name's Mike Hammer. That mean anything to you?"

"…I thought you looked familiar."

"I'm going to send a replacement fare out to you as soon as I can. You're to drive him to the Hackard Building. He'll pay the freight."

"This is way more complicated than 'follow that car.'"

"Yeah, but I just know you're up to it, since there'll be a five-buck tip in it."

I could hear the shrug in his voice. "Why not?"

Now I looked around the station house reception area. A guy about my age and size in a raincoat was lodging a complaint against his landlord. I listened to him not get anywhere with the desk sergeant, and when I went up to him his face was red with anger. Seemed like perfect casting to me.

"You want to make a quick fifty?" I asked him.

"Who do I have to kill?" Not the smartest thing to say in a police station, but nobody but me was listening.

I explained that he was to run out of here, fast, take that waiting cab across the street, and pay for the fare and a five buck tip out of a twenty I'd give him.

"Go inside the Hackard Building," I said, "wait a couple minutes, then go back out through the coffee shop entrance and take a cab home or wherever the rest of that twenty will take you."

"I got it," he said, nodding. "So where's the fifty?"

I gave him a beautiful crisp engraving of President Grant.

The guy was heading out, then turned and called, "What's this all about, anyway?"

"It's about you making fifty bucks," I said.

That was good enough for him.

I lagged back in the niche of the doorway. In the quick exit to the cab from the building, the guy could have passed for me. I watched the cab pull away. Right behind, a new black Ford with two men in the front seat pulled out and fell in line.

I jotted down the plate number, and sent a note up to Pat, asking him to check it out with the Motor Vehicle Bureau. Then I took a side door just past the locker room out to the street.

Fifteen minutes later, using a wall pay phone in a small gin mill on Eighth Avenue, I called Pat. He came on the line with a grunt, and said, "So where'd you come up with that plate number, Mike?"

I told him about the stunt with the cab.

"You're getting cute in your old age, buddy. Let's hope you didn't get some poor schlub killed because he was wearing a raincoat and got out at the Hackard Building."

"If so, it'll be a relief to that landlord he was bitching about. What about those wheels?"

"Stolen vehicle. If you think that car is full of guys with guns, I can put out an APB."

"Do that."

"Anything to please a tax payer."

"Pat..."

"What?"

"That car was outside your station house. That means my Russian friends know you're in this, too. That we're friends. Watch your ass."

"Not a problem. My ass is in a sling thanks to you, and that makes it easy to keep an eye on."

He hung up.

I used another dime to buzz the Blue Ribbon and Angie said Des Casey had called and left me a phone number that I recognized as that of Peerage Brokers on Broadway.

The front for Rickerby's New York office.

"Your friend said it was urgent, Mike," Angie said.

"Thanks, Angie," I said, and put the phone back.

Everything was urgent with feds, except getting your tax refund back to you.

I had other things to do, and they could take their damn turn.

The Wentworth Hotel's rooms were either high-end residential or permanently reserved by regular wealthy patrons who couldn't be bothered with the inconvenience of arranging lodgings or packing luggage on a trip to the city. It boasted neither marquee nor doorman, and announced its existence only by way of a small bronze plaque set into the brick beside the entrance.

But once inside you realized its exclusiveness. You were visually inspected, your credentials requested, your presence announced by desk phone, and if found acceptable, you were escorted by private elevator to the appropriate apartment in the company of a cold, quietly contemptuous staff member, who delivered you like a package to the door of the guest or resident, not leaving until that staff member ascertained that you were indeed expected.

And yet all of this exclusivity and security had not prevented Pietro Romanos from crashing the senator's party the night that started it all....

Irene Carroll thanked the assistant manager, who was so pompous that a tip would have offended him, and he went away.

She stood there, posed in the doorway as if she were a picture and it were her frame, rather boldly outfitted in a Chinese-looking pair of silk lounging pajamas, sky blue with white trimmings, the tips of her full breasts apparent under the fabric. Her feet were bare.

"I was wondering when you would come around, Mike."

"Surprised?"

"Pleasantly so. Oh, I expected you to take me up on my invitation, just not so soon."

She turned sideways and gestured for me to come in. I did, brushing by her. She closed the door behind me and I moved through a rather blank entryway into a living room where I expected to find fine old original oil paintings and carefully selected antique furniture.

There were originals here, all right, but of the blown-up comic-book panel and giant soup can variety. The walls and carpet were white, and the furniture geometric, solid blues and reds. I doubted these mod trimmings had come with a Wentworth apartment, and wondered if all the red, white and blue was meant to be patriotic, or was that just a pop art accident?

"Now *I've* surprised *you*," she said, smiling, arms folded on the shelf of her generous bosom.

"Not what I pictured," I admitted.

She sat down on a blue sofa and motioned with a sweep of her hand for me to take the red chair opposite her. When she crossed her legs, there was a sensual swish of silk. That magnificent body was completely covered, but the nakedness beneath the draped fabric taunted me.

"My home in Georgetown," she said, with a regal shake of her sleek chin-cut white hair, "is painfully, properly Early American. Frankly, to call it a home is a disservice… it's a mansion. Lovely, tasteful, and filled with antiques that many a museum would envy."

"So when you come to the city, you like a change."

She shrugged. "I come here to have a good time. I don't throw the parties, I just go to them." She smiled to herself, laughed the same way, then shared her thoughts: "My late husband oversaw the decoration of the Georgetown place. He would have a *shit* fit if he saw this. Particularly if he knew how much that Warhol cost, and those Lichtensteins."

I smiled and nodded, like I knew what the hell she was talking about, then said, "You mentioned you might be able to help me with my current… situation."

"Your… *situation*, Mike, as you so euphemistically put it, has Washington in an uproar… and, in some respects, of course, I *am* Washington."

"And here I thought *I* had an ego."

"Not ego, Mike, rather hard reality. There are times when my services are essential in that town. Politics are not entirely made in smoke-filled caucus rooms, you know."

"So I've heard," I said. "But I try to stay out of politics."

"Lately you have a funny way of doing that, Mike."

"Politics is Republicans and Democrats, and I couldn't have less interest in either. But when a bunch of slobs have world domination in mind, this old G.I. sits up and takes notice. Because that's about survival, and survival's a subject I'm an expert in."

She got her lovely, strange laugh going again, and I started to bristle, and she saw that. Her laughter stopped, her expression grew more serious, and she held her palms up in surrender.

"I don't mean to offend you, Mike. I'm not laughing at you."

"Well, you're not laughing *with* me, lady, 'cause I'm not laughing."

"Now I *have* offended you. I'm sorry. So very sorry. I laugh because you are so impressive, such a rare example of the kind of man you rarely seen anymore."

"Try a museum. Ancient history wing."

"Mike… I'm interested in you. My meeting you this morning wasn't entirely born of curiosity. It was suggested by certain people that I arrange to see you, draw you out, even get… *close* to you… and report back what I had learned."

"You'd be taking on some hard duty, kid."

That got a sudden smile and that tinkly laugh again. "Yes, I'm beginning to figure that out. I took the time to read up on you and ask a few discreet questions. That's why I'm being so frank."

"Think you can learn more that way?"

"Possibly," she admitted. "But after spending even a little time with you, I don't expect you to tell me any more than you *want* me to know… so now it's back to a matter of curiosity again."

She flipped open an enameled box and held it out to me. "Cigarette?"

They were black with gold tips. "No. I gave that up. Too risky."

That got a laugh out of her, that tinkling thing that was two parts bells ringing and one part breaking glass. She selected a cigarette, produced a small lighter from somewhere, then sat back smoking with her arms crossed under her breasts, lifting them, a pose that was intentionally provocative.

I made a gesture with my shoulders and relaxed in the chair. The damn thing was actually pretty comfortable. "You were supposed to have been at Allen's party the night the shooting took place."

"Thank goodness I was late!"

"Yeah, thank goodness," I said. I was starting to wonder about that. "You knew everybody on the guest list, didn't you?"

"Certainly. Quite well. Some were people of importance, others simply friends of Allen's. It was a kind of going-away party for Allen, you know, with the Russian trip coming up shortly. It was a last-minute affair on his part and there wasn't time for him and his wife... do you know Emily?"

"Yes, I met her. Nice lady."

"Wonderful woman. One of the sweetest you could hope to meet... Anyway, it was too late for the Jaspers to arrange anything very elaborate. I think they got the idea of putting together a party the week before, when N.A.S.A. threw their own party after the successful Gadfly launch. Allen and Emily went down to be part of that, you know. He's a big supporter of N.A.S.A., which isn't the case with every senator of his political persuasion. He went down there in part as a show of support for his friend, Dr. Giles—Harmon Giles... whom I believe you know."

"Not well. He patched me up that night."

She looked skyward, as if she could see the satellites spinning up there. "Harmon Giles is one of the modern greats."

"Really."

"Oh yes, he was in the aerospace program as a surgeon-scientist since its inception. Overwork forced his retirement, and he went back to private practice after the last launch. They still call him in for consultations."

"I might check in with him myself. Leg is still buggin' me a little."

Her smile was teasing. "Hope it's nothing too *serious*…?"

I smiled back at her. "Doesn't interfere with anything important."

She gave me a sleepy-lidded glance. "No, I wouldn't imagine so."

"How about filling me in on the other guests?"

"You really should talk to Allen about them."

"I want your version."

She took a deep drag on the cigarette, blew smoke out through dragon nostrils, and snuffed it out in a red enamel ashtray.

Finally, she said, "I don't know what you're looking for, Mike, but I do know this: most of the guests had security clearances, and the others were all personal friends of Allen's. Allen would never associate with anyone disreputable or suspect in any way. He's a fine man, a fine American, and he's my friend."

I didn't remember suggesting otherwise. Why was she defensive all of a sudden?

"Anyway," she was saying, the moment gone now, "my understanding is that the shooting you were involved in grew out of an attempted robbery."

"It could have been something else."

Her eyes tensed. "What?"

"Assassination."

"Of whom?"

"That's what I'm wondering about."

"Of *Allen*?" She leaned forward, watching me as if she feared I might make a break for it. "Doubtful, Mike. Doubtful."

"Why?"

"Allen is a controversial figure, at times, but he doesn't have *those* kinds of enemy. Somebody might toss an egg, but not a…"

"Bullet? Irene, he's a United States senator. All it takes is one screwball—one disgruntled, homicidal constituent. You said *other* important people were there."

"Not of a similar stature. Anyone else there could have been replaced in their role by someone equally as competent."

"What about Dr. Giles?"

She shook her head, the white hair shimmering. "Why attack a retired space program surgeon?"

"Did you ever consider this?" I asked, sitting forward. "*You* were supposed to have been there too. You didn't show up until after it was over."

Alarm dawned. "You mean, *I* could have been…"

"The target? Yes. If it *was* an assassination attempt, why not you? You *are* Washington, remember?"

"I meant that tongue-in-cheek, Mike!" Speaking of her tongue, it touched her lips and left them gleaming wetly. "I'm just a… a glorified *hostess*…"

"You're the only one left of your kind in Washington and you damn well know it. With your contacts, you could have heard or seen something you weren't supposed to, and if you ever put the pieces together, and exposed this knowledge, it might have national or even international ramifications."

"That is just *ridiculous*." But even as she said it, her voice was shaking and her tone weak.

"*Is* it?" I asked quietly.

"Mike…"

"Think about it, Irene. This began the night you were late to a party. Everyone figures your jewels are a possible motive. But maybe it was your life that guy was after."

She let her hands fall into her lap and I saw the machinery of her mind going into motion. She threw back a stray lock of hair and said, "You were the one abducted, Mike. In Russia. Not Manhattan."

"Right now, Irene, the heat's on me because Soviet national prestige is on the line. But let's assume that you *are* an unwitting part of this… that you *do* know something, even if you don't recognize it, much less remember it."

"Mike, you're scaring me…"

"My showing up at that party was something Allen didn't even know about till the last minute. I *could* have been there to make contact with you per your instructions. I have certain things in my background that would come in handy if you needed a strong defender in dealing with the Soviets."

"Oh, but you *know* it wasn't like that."

"But does the K.G.B. know it, Irene?"

She got up suddenly, tossed her hair and went to a small

black-and-white bar in the corner and made a drink. I shook my head when she offered me one. When she walked over, her nervousness was palpable. "What you suggest just isn't possible."

"Oh, it's possible," I said. "Now I need to determine if it's probable."

"I wish you hadn't even mentioned it…"

I got up and reached for my hat. "Had to, honey. I needed to see your reaction."

"You saw it. And?"

"And I'm satisfied. If this starts to look like you were the catalyst, I'll be in touch straightaway."

She put her drink down on the glass coffee table and almost ran to me. "Mike—please don't go. Not yet."

"You'll be all right here," I told her. "The President couldn't get in this damn hotel without getting patted down and grilled. But if you want me to put a man outside, I can arrange that."

Her arms snaked around me and her fingers were at my neck, one hand digging into the hair at the nape. "Please stay, Mike…" She pressed against me and the warmth of her body wanted to suck me in like a vacuum. The apparent softness was all firm reality, her heavy breathing giving a separate and deliberate movement to her thighs and the flat of her belly.

This was a woman. Not a little girl. A woman with curves and flesh and passion and urgency…

I hugged her lightly, then held her away. "There's too much to be done for me to stay," I said. "I'll be back, Irene. I will be back."

She stepped away reluctantly. "That wasn't right, throwing a scare into me like that."

"Why not, honey?" I grinned at her. "You scare the hell out of me."

A flicker of a smile parted her lips. "All right. Get out of here, you big bully. And I'll work at thinking up ways to scare you even better."

"I just might like that," I said.

And I stuffed on my hat and left her in the red, white and blue living room, with the big comic-book face of a crying woman staring at her.

Peerage Brokers was a single floor in an unremarkable building on Broadway. It could have been an accounting firm or a mail order company or anything at all, really, with its desks and chairs and filing cabinets and typewriters and faceless crew of apparent office drones. But this was a very different kind of business, behind the bland façade.

The brunette receptionist was in her thirties, neither attractive nor unattractive, in a gray suit. Unlike Jasper's secretary, she didn't pretend not to know me.

"Mr. Rickerby's in the conference room, Mr. Hammer."

"Thanks, kiddo."

Art Rickerby was standing facing a window, waiting for me, with Tony Wale already seated at a small conference table. Another guy was seated there, too. Him I didn't recognize. This struck me as a roadshow version of my recent farce in D.C.—call it *The Pentagon Follies*. I shut the door behind me. Art turned and motioned me toward a chair.

The stranger sat at the head of the table—a slim, narrow-faced guy in a three-piece suit, his hair short and gray, with frozen gray eyes that dissected me as I walked over and sat down and tossed my hat on the table.

The guy didn't bother to get up or offer a hand to shake when Rickerby said, "Vincent Worth, Mike Hammer."

Rickerby sat, leaving one chair between us. "Mike, Mr. Worth is attached to Special Sections."

I gave the great Mr. Worth the most sneeringly insolent expression I could muster.

"Mr. Worth can drop dead," I said.

With as much expression as Buster Keaton regarding a train coming his way, Worth said, "I've heard about your childish attitude, Hammer."

"Mike," Rickerby said, "Mr. Worth is in charge of this case now. There are multiple agencies involved, including mine, and Mr. Worth is coordinating all of their efforts."

Worth said, "Cooperation is not optional, Hammer."

I sat forward. "Who the hell do you think you're screwing with? Any cooperation you get from me is a matter of my own choice and discretion, so don't give me any crap and maybe I'll play ball. *Maybe*. Now—what urgent thing did you want to see me about?"

I'll give them credit, Worth particularly. My little tantrum didn't faze any of them. Rickerby and Wale had heard it all before, and this newcomer of a scrawny unblinking bureaucrat had been told what to expect.

Worth said, "Our orders were to go along with you only so far, Hammer. Don't press your luck."

"Why not?"

"Because your odds of making it to the end of the week are just about nil without *our* cooperation."

Something clearly was up—Rickerby's expression sent that message, strong. So it was time to lean back and shut up and behave.

Worth reached in a coat pocket and tugged out an envelope. He tossed it on the table like the card that won the game. "We got a make on that print your secretary lifted in your office yesterday."

I frowned. "Was it the guy who killed the real Rath?"

"We don't know if your visitor did the actual killing or not. That was likely someone else. We just know who your *visitor* was… is. The report came in from London a few hours ago."

"I'm interested."

"Felipe Mandau—a known Soviet agent."

In spy speak, that wasn't redundant—that Mandau was a "known" Soviet agent and not just a "suspected" one was significant.

"So," I said, "you have definitive proof that a K.G.B. agent is operating on American soil."

"We do, Mr. Hammer."

It was "Mr. Hammer," again. We were regular lodge members now.

Worth was saying, "Mandau works exclusively on high-priority, special assignments. We know he was implicated in that Canadian business a few years ago, and again in Madrid earlier this year. There are no useful pictures of him, nor any positive physical identification."

"Why's that?"

Rickerby chimed in: "This spook works the disguise bit. He's a master at it."

Worth went on: "Your description of him is of little or no value because it's unlikely that he'll appear the same the next time."

Then that froggy look of his had been stagecraft. You had to be damn good to pull that kind of thing off at close quarters.

"So I may not recognize him myself," I said, "should I run into him."

"That's right. And we're sharing this information with you, Mr. Hammer, because Mandau's interest in you is... suggestive."

"Of what?"

Rickerby said, "As Mr. Worth said before, Mike, this assassin only works high-priority assignments. That confirms our assumptions that you are a top K.G.B. target."

"And you already know why," I said. "Right now, the Soviets look like saps, and I'm the guy who—"

Worth cut me off. "Perhaps there's a different reason, Mr. Hammer. We believe that K.G.B. agents or domestic assets may have had several opportunities to kill you since your return to New York."

"I'm not that easy to kill."

Rickerby said, "Damnit, Mike, quit being so full of yourself. You *really* think the K.G.B. couldn't liquidate one lousy private eye if they felt like it?"

"They couldn't manage it back home. What makes you think they can pull it off on my turf?"

Worth said, "Hasn't it occurred to you, Mr. Hammer, that

Mandau could have taken out both you and your secretary before Sergeant Casey slugged him?"

"He didn't have time," I said.

But who was I kidding? He did just stand there a while…

Rickerby said, "We're inclined to think there's another reason why you weren't shot down in cold blood."

"Look, guys…"

"*You* look, Hammer. Felipe Mandau is the likely assassin on half a dozen major hits internationally in the last two-and-a-half years. The K.G.B. isn't likely to waste his considerable talents on an inconsequential subject. Ever hear of Conrad Toy?"

"No."

"Then I'll enlighten you. Conrad Toy is Colonel Toyevshka, only the man largely responsible for disrupting the unity between the Allies after World War II. When Drushev was ousted, Toy took over the K.G.B. department designed to blow Latin American relations wide open, and he damn near succeeded. Despite our putting a crimp in those plans, he managed to avoid shipment to a gulag during the recent regime change. He is reportedly now in charge of international assassinations."

Rickerby said, "Conrad Toy is Felipe Mandau's direct superior, and we have reports that he may be in the country. Possibly in this city."

Worth picked up: "And when they go so far out on a limb as to put the likes of Toy on the scene in person? You *know* the situation's hot."

"So catch him," I said with a shrug. "All you alphabet boys are in the soup together on this one, aren't you?"

"We will catch him," Worth told me slowly, "but probably not until we find out where you come into this."

"What, do you think I'm holding out? Hell, technically I'm one of Rickerby's men—you want to see my badge?"

"Mike," Rickerby said, "we just think there's something else *to* this, something we don't know, and something *you* don't know."

"No, I *do* know," I said.

They all sat forward, even the frozen-eyed Worth.

"If they've passed up chances to kill me," I said, "that means they want me alive. They want to abduct me again. Make me stand trial in Moscow. Embarrass Uncle Sam and make me out a war criminal."

Rickerby and Worth exchanged glances. Across the table sat Tony Wale. He hadn't said a word throughout all of this.

I said, "I gave you guys the picture loud and clear in Washington. You read the polygraph charts. What else do you want from me?"

Worth looked at Rickerby and nodded.

Then Rickerby, with a smile that wouldn't fool an infant, said, "Frankly, Mike, we'd like to dangle you out there as bait."

"Aren't you doing that already?"

"You have a minimum amount of support on this thing—Sergeant Casey at your side, and a handful of agents salted around keeping an eye on you and… Velda."

There was something in Rickerby's voice I didn't like. "Why the pause before Velda's name?"

And now, finally, Tony Wale spoke.

He and I went way back, but he had done damn little to help me when I was held in D.C.

"You're very close to your secretary, aren't you?" Wale said. "She's a remarkable woman, Miss Sterling."

I felt the muscles in my upper back go taut. "Yeah, she is. So what?"

"An hour ago we prevented her attempted abduction. The two men who tried it were killed."

I reached across the table and grabbed him by his lapels and dragged him over to me. The other two men jumped from their chairs, startled as hell.

"Where *is* she, Tony?"

He was scared, flopping on that table like a swordfish on deck; his hands clutched at my wrists and tried to force them down, but he couldn't. "Take it easy, Mike! She's home! Home and safe."

I let go slowly, then clenched my fists again so they couldn't see my hands trembling. Wale crawled back across the table, shaken and missing his dignity.

I turned to Rickerby. "Who were they, Art?"

"Local hoods. One of our cars cut them off, and the punks knew they'd been had. There was a high-speed chase and they turned their car over. Both died in the crash."

"That's too bad."

"Yes. We would have liked to question them."

"I would have liked to break their necks."

Worth said, "Mr. Hammer, we don't believe your secretary knew the attempt was even made. They were spotted moving in, saw our people, and panicked, trying to get out of it. That simple. You were lucky we were tagging along behind her. Right now, we're running a check on both the late perpetrators, but I'm not holding out any hopes of finding anything."

"Damn!"

Rickerby said, "Mike, this tells us they're reaching out to locals—that means they have a limited crew here in the States. We've picked up back-channel chatter that indicates a second assassin, possibly Mandau's partner, is also in the country."

I smashed a fist into my palm. There were lightning flashes in front of my eyes. "I'll find them all and I'll kill them all!"

"Actually, Mike," Rickerby said, "you're closer to what we're after than you might guess."

"Huh? What?"

Worth said, "The pressure's on in Washington, Mr. Hammer. Tomorrow the Soviet Ambassador is making a visit to the White House. There are voices against you in both houses of Congress, and Communist factions around the world are screaming for your hide."

I made a suggestion about what all these good people could do to themselves.

Rickerby was in the chair next to me now. He put a hand on my shoulder. "There is a real problem tied into all this, Mike, and it's a bad one."

My head was throbbing. "And the hits just keep on coming. *What?*"

His voice was as calm as mine was ragged. "As you pointed out back in D.C., we don't have any extradition agreement with Soviet Russia... but we *do* have such treaties with several of those other countries you, uh, traveled through."

"Aw, shit."

"You can come out on the short end, my friend."

I took a deep breath, then let it out slowly. "I can hear it in your voice, Ricketyback… you've got an angle."

The three men exchanged glances, and tiny smiles. I didn't know whether to be nervous or reassured.

"Mike, if you can deliver one of those Soviet agents to us, preferably alive," Rickerby said, "we would have evidence of espionage on American soil. That could be viewed as an act of war."

"Or," Worth said, "it could serve as a bargaining chip."

"I give you a K.G.B. agent," I said, "and you can put the squeeze on the Soviets?"

"We can trade someone on the level of Mandau or even better Conrad Toy for half a dozen of our people rotting in an East Berlin prison."

"And part of the deal is the heat comes off me?"

Rickerby nodded. "You have our word. You have *my* word."

I rolled that around in my mind some. "How much time have I got?"

Worth said, "These efforts to extradite you have to go through all sorts of channels, of course. I'd say you might have a week. That is, if you can live that long, or avoid being abducted. Of course, if you would allow us to increase our protective *participation*…"

"No," I said, and reached for my hat. I got to my feet. "I don't want to scare these boys off. Now we're at the flush them out stage."

"Otherwise, Mr. Hammer," Worth said, "if this extradition effort goes through, I would get a really top-notch lawyer, if I were you."

"Oh, if it comes up," I said, "I'll get the best."

"That's a relief to hear." He paused and frowned. "Who might that be?"

"The American public," I said. "I want to see what the voters will do to the idiots who yelled for my scalp."

CHAPTER NINE

Des Casey was waiting for me in the Peerage Brokers reception area, a soldier uncomfortably out of uniform. Beyond his attitude, the only thing G.I. about him was his shoes and socks. For some reason, career guys never seem to change those when they get into civvies.

Down on the street, we caught a cab and climbed in. Since Rickerby had used him to summon me, Casey seemed apologetic when he asked, "They give you a rough time up there?"

"It'll get rougher."

His shook his head and his eyes widened. "Brother, did they lay into me for letting you take off alone." He handed me a small notebook and said, "I think I got most of the information you were looking for. Didn't take that long."

"How did the senator come out?"

"Clean, Mike. As close to spotless as I figure any politician *could* be. He has no suspicious business ties, has cut himself off from any of the proceeds from his law firm while he's in office, and he's known for voting his conscience… even when it's at odds with campaign donors."

"You said 'close to spotless.'"

His grin had a nice boyish quality, surprising from such a rugged guy. "Well, I don't have anything to support that, but your friend Hy Gardner told me there were… how did he put it? 'Whispers' about Jasper's personal life. Mr. Gardner said if you wanted to know more, you should stop by his office in person."

"That sounds like Hy. Okay, I'll do that."

"What next?"

"How are your contacts around this town?"

"They go back a few years. But I still got 'em."

"Good. See what you can get on a deceased punk named Pietro Romanos."

I gave him everything Pat had passed on to me. That he'd been out of the loop for a while actually gave Casey a certain advantage. His military status overshadowed any of his police background, and a G.I. on leave can get into all kinds of places no questions asked. And there was always the excuse of looking up an old buddy, if somebody asked—after a couple of belts of booze, those old-line infantrymen will always talk up a storm with one of their own.

"Listen," I said, "act like you don't know Romanos is dead. Say that he's a longtime pal you're trying to get in touch with. When you ask somebody about somebody who turns out to be dead, all kinds of information comes pouring out."

"How would I have known Romanos?"

"Des, you've got the perfect excuse to reach out to him. This Romanos was a competition sharp shooter. You took several division championship pistol matches, right?"

"Right."

"Isn't it conceivable that at one time or another, you went up against Romanos at a meet?"

"It is. You're pretty good at this detective stuff, aren't you, Mike?"

"Yeah. I gotta be." I grinned at him. "The killing evil bastards part doesn't pay that well."

The kid thought that was pretty funny, but the cabbie was frowning at us in the rearview mirror.

"Then, Mike, you want me to go off on my own again?"

"I do. But it's strictly volunteer. I can't promise I can protect your stripes, son."

"I never wanted to be a sergeant forever, anyway."

Two blocks from our apartment building, I got out, waited for the cab's taillights to disappear around the corner, then started to walk west. The drizzle that had greased the streets stopped momentarily, then the wind came back with a soft chill to it and the rain began with that strange quality of blanketing the sounds that were the heartbeat of the city.

I didn't see them, but I knew they were there. Field glasses would be trained on anyone entering the apartment building and the doorman standing out of the wet wasn't the same one I had seen last time. Neither was the porter who was making a sad show of emptying clean ashtrays into a pail in the lobby. God bless 'em, they couldn't hide it. There was too much training there. They looked at me casually, nodded half-heartedly, playing the game to the hilt, but they might as well have left their badges pinned to their shirts.

I went on upstairs to two floors above Velda's, pushed the down button and reached in to punch the floor before the doors closed, then took the stairs. In the lobby, they'd be watching the floor pointer above the elevator doors and wondering what the hell that was all about. It'd break the monotony for them a little bit.

My coded knock didn't get a response right away, and I was just getting worried when she answered the door in a short baby-blue terrycloth robe, in the process of towel-drying all that raven's wing hair. She grinned at me as I stood there taking all of her in, then said, "Stop breathing through your mouth, Mike, and come on in."

I did, and she shut the door and bolted it. There was no fear in her—we were in a hopeless situation, but we'd been in those before. Any concern in her now would be for me. And the same was true of me for her.

When she took my hand and squeezed it, I knew she knew about the attempt to abduct her.

"Who told you, Velda?"

"Pat called me. Come over and sit with me on the couch…"

Her apartment was small and homey, inviting in its soft colors and comfortable furnishings. Nothing about it indicated the remarkable woman who lived here, not unless you started opening drawers and looking in this decorative box and that apparent humidor and saw the four .32s salted around the little living room.

She curled up on the couch with her legs under her. I sat beside her with my arm along the back cushions.

"Pat didn't get any official confirmation," she said. "The NYPD just had an accident fatality report come in, and those get run past Homicide. Pat noticed the address and put two and two together. But he really added it up after he saw the names on the sheet of those men working out of Washington."

"Okay, Rickerby's crew had your back, and good for them. But from here on out you stay put."

"No way," she said fiercely. "I'm in this as deep as you are."

"I'm still your boss."

"I'm your partner. There's a difference." She shifted her bottom a little and leaned my way, some edge in her voice. "I knew damn well I was being tailed by our people, and it didn't bother me. If I'd wanted to shake them... well, you taught me some pretty fancy tricks and I've picked up a few on my own."

"No dice. You're grounded."

"Damnit! What happened today shows that they have me covered just fine! You are one stubborn... *damn* you, sometimes!"

When she got mad, she got even more beautiful. Her dark eyes danced with a peculiar sparkle and those lovely breasts heaved with the heat of her anger. I grinned at her and before she could protest, I moved in, my arms around her, my mouth on hers, tasting all that loveliness until she was just a breathless bundle of female who could only say, "You may know how to shut me up, Mike... but you still lost the argument."

"This is losing?"

She kissed me. It wasn't just a kiss, not when her tongue went searching for the back of my throat. Then she asked, "Am I still grounded, Daddy?"

"...No."

"Turns out Mike Hammer *can* be bribed."

"Not with money." I eased away from her. "Now, can we talk a little business?"

She leaned toward me. "Why don't you finish what you started first…"

"Turn off your switch."

"I can't."

"Why not?"

"I can't find it. Why don't *you* look for it…"

I backed away. "Later, baby. Business, first."

"Okay. Your loss."

"Be useful, why don't you? Get us a couple of beers."

She gave me a Sieg Heil salute and got off the couch, flashing some skin under that terrycloth robe, making me want to reconsider or maybe kick myself. All those months were still racked up inside me and I wanted her so bad that the hurt was as physical as it was emotional.

She brought back two Blue Ribbons and I drained half of mine with a single gulp and set the can down. For ten minutes I brought her up to date, then said, "How about your end?"

"How about my end?"

"Be good."

Her handbag was on the nearby coffee table and she snapped it open and got out several folded sheets of paper. She passed them to me.

"Here's what I found on the senator's partygoers," she said. "I didn't come up with anything suspicious much less dirty. Jasper's friends have everything from A-1 credit ratings to security clearances. The only one I had trouble with was the Contreaux woman."

I glanced from the sheets. "Why?"

"For one thing, when I spoke to her briefly at her apartment today, she was polite but not terribly forthcoming."

"There's something else?"

Velda nodded. "She's Dr. Giles' assistant and personal secretary, and they are both engaged in classified work on various space projects."

"But he's retired."

"Yes, but he's still doing liaison work when necessary, and has a top security rating. Still doing research at Manheim University, too, who don't like inquiries into their staff. Or at least not into their government-funded projects."

"So you came up empty on the Contreaux doll?"

"No, I got everything," she said, "it just wasn't that easy." She was gesturing to the papers in my hands. "Keep looking, you'll see. With the senator backing you up, they finally gave me everything I asked for."

"Maybe I need to dig a little deeper."

"No!"

She said it so fast and hard that it knocked me off balance. Then she smiled and laughed a little.

"Okay, so you caught me," she said. "You called her a 'doll,' and you're not wrong. She's a little too beautiful for me to send you out there investigating her, uh… background."

"*She's* too beautiful? Ever look in the mirror, kid?"

"Even if the mirror says I'm still the fairest in the land, that girl's got something, Mike, and you damn well know it."

"I'm just trying to be thorough."

"You be thorough with me," she said, with a minxy little smile.

"Anyway, you met her at the party, didn't you?"

"Yeah, but just briefly. I was there to do a job, not mingle with the guests."

"But she accompanied you with Dr. Giles to his office, to patch you up."

"Did she? After I caught that slug, I wasn't too interested in 'dolls.' What can you tell me about Lisa Contreaux?"

"That I hate her."

"Quit kidding."

"Who's kidding?" She sighed and folded her arms over her bosom. "All right. She's twenty-nine, has a doctorate in physics and has been with Harmon Giles two years. Apparently she has an important position, is well-liked, well-respected, and attends to Dr. Giles' needs."

"All of them?"

"Keeping in mind the age difference of twenty-some years, I doubt that."

"Some of us old guys still got some spunk left, kitten."

"I know all about your spunk, big boy." She dug her elbow in my ribs. "To be fair, when I said she wasn't forthcoming, I should have cut her some slack. She is, after all, in mourning."

"What do you mean?"

"Well, her fiancé died, recently—apparently a nice innocuous young scientist… It's in my notes. Dennis Dorfman. He worked with Dr. Perry Gleason in Organic Science Studies at Manheim."

I was sitting up now. "How did the Dorfman boy die? He was just a kid, so don't tell me natural causes."

"Well, it's natural to die when you get run over by a Buick."

"Don't tell me—hit-and-run driver."

"Yeah. Just about a week ago. And before you bite my head off, I checked with Pat. It went down near the campus. Witnesses saw a college-age kid behind the wheel of what turned out to be a stolen car. Appears to be a joy ride that turned tragic."

"And the driver has never been found."

"No, Mike. Pat said there was one little odd thing about it."

"Yeah?"

"The kid's last words. Young Dorfman was unconscious at the scene, badly injured, but he came around when they were loading him in the ambulance. He died on the way to the hospital."

"What did he say, Vel?"

"He said… 'Complex 90.' He said it several times, apparently. The ambulance attendants said he was grabbing one of their shirts when he said it for the last time, right before he passed out again. In minutes he was gone."

"Complex 90…"

"Does that mean anything to you, Mike?"

"No. How about you?"

"No. Not a thing. Now, *that* might be worth asking Lisa Contreaux about, at that. I can do it for you, Mike, tomorrow…"

"I'll handle it. I'm capable of talking to a beautiful woman without becoming a crazed sex fiend, you know."

"Yeah, well the jury's out on that one. Oh, speaking of Pat and stolen cars, he said the vehicle with those plates you called in— the one you sent on a wild goose chase? It was found abandoned on the East Side."

"Did they dust it for prints?"

"They hadn't yet when I talked to him. He said the car was being towed over to the city garage, where a forensics team would be waiting."

I was sitting there brooding, so she got up, got me another Blue Ribbon, and sat back down to patiently wait for me to process everything she'd told me.

"What else?" I said finally.

"I didn't talk to this Harmon Giles in person," Velda said, picking right up. "I think maybe you should check in with him."

"Right, if nothing more than to ask him for some painkillers. He may be a hot shit with N.A.S.A., but he did a lousy job on my leg."

"So complain to him in person. You were lucky he was there. He has a reputation for being one of the best surgeons in the country."

"You could have fooled me. Anything interesting on the other guests?"

She gave that a little thought, then said, "Well, apparently this Wall Street whiz, who was to have been Irene Carroll's date that night… Warren Bentley? Word is an engagement is imminent."

"Somehow I doubt that."

"Why?"

"Call it a hunch." I decided not to tell her about earlier, when Irene Carroll pressed herself to me like a suction cup on glass.

"Velda, could any of that crowd, besides the senator himself, have been important enough to rate an assassination attempt?"

"Maybe Dr. Giles." She touched the tip of my nose with a forefinger. "Or you, Mike. You do have a few enemies left alive. Not all of them are behind the Iron Curtain, either."

I sipped the beer, shook my head. "It all begins with that party at Jasper's penthouse pad. The cops figured it a botched jewelry heist, but it was something else."

"How odd," she said, frowning, but also laughing a strange little laugh.

"What is?"

"That *that's* what led to you winding up on the run in Russia. When the same damn thing happened to me…"

During the war, when she was an agent with the O.S.S., Velda had been part of the effort to break up Butterfly Two, a freelance espionage ring that dated back to the early twenties, headed up by one Gerald Erlich. Butterfly Two had offered its services to the highest bidder, and Hitler's Germany had won. No Nazi himself, just a hard-bitten, cold-eyed pro, Erlich disappeared post-war with all his accumulated wealth, and the Reds swallowed up the spy ring.

Less than a decade later, in New York, independently wealthy Rudolph Civic became known as a generous donor to charity and the arts as well as a prominent contributor to local political campaigns. His wife made frequent appearances on the society pages, but Civic himself was known to be camera-shy. Not surprising, given that Civic was Gerald Erlich, hiding behind a new, respectable identity.

Knowing nothing of this, I got hired on a routine security job for a society event of Civic's that I sent Velda to handle. Dressed to the nines like just another jet setter, Velda could mingle more effectively than me and even follow Mrs. Civic and her fabulous gems into the powder room.

A routine enough job... until the host made a late arrival at his own party, and the two former spies, Velda and Civic, recognized each other at once. They had a tense confab in the midst of clinking cocktails glasses and brittle laughter, the former Erlich assuming Velda had tracked him down, Velda assuming Civic had lured her there. Either might have mistakenly shot the other had fate not intervened. In the bedroom where Civic and his wife had gone to freshen up, with bodyguard Velda in attendance, a gang of Red agents posing as jewel thieves broke in and abducted all three, emptying the safe of its valuable stones.

The next day, Civic's wife, a pudgy dame, was found in the river with her fat fingers severed to allow the removal of the precious gems she wore. This convinced the cops—and me, at the time—that this was a heist gone horribly wrong, the work of uncommonly vicious thieves.

In reality, Civic and Velda were smuggled out of the country and wound up prisoners in central Europe. Civic, actually Gerald Erlich, was considered a very dangerous loose end by the Kremlin, since every major agent he'd employed was now working for the Soviets—the names, the identities, even the places inside his head made him valuable... and dangerous. Somehow Civic and Velda slipped their captors and made their own inside-Russia escape, and the chase was on. The two pooled their resources and information, and were on the run for an incredible seven years. Civic they killed. Velda made it back.

A lot of the details I didn't know. As close as Velda and I were, two factors had kept me from asking her a thousand questions—first, this had been a government mission, an ex-agent called back into service by unforeseen events, and much of what happened was simply not my business. Second, she had a right to her privacy. She would tell me what she wanted to, and hold back what she wanted to. I understood. I was fine with it. All I had ever wanted was her back in my life. I had spent seven years inside a bottle because she was dead. When she turned up alive, I wasn't interested in the fine print.

"Now," she said with a shudder, cuddled close to me on the couch, my arm around her terrycloth-covered shoulders, "after all these years… the damn Soviets again."

"But we have a ticket out of this mess."

She nodded. "Turn over one live K.G.B. agent, and your friend Rickerby has the bargaining power with the Kremlin to get you taken off the big hit list."

"And to swap some of our guys out of East Berlin stir."

"We've both been in prison over there now, Mike. We both know what it means to get out."

"Well, my stay wasn't very long, sugar."

"Nor mine. I never told you, but… I'm sure they *let* us escape."

"You and Rudy Civic, you mean?"

"Yes. We all but waltzed out of there, nothing like what you had to pull off. They thought Civic would lead them to agents of theirs, former agents of his, that they couldn't trust."

"But you shook them. You shook them off."

She nodded. She was trembling. "Mike. Mike, I love you."

"Well, I love you, baby."

"There's something… something I never told you. About what happened over there. To me."

"You don't have to."

"You should know. There's something… important."

"The past isn't important."

"This part of it is… Mike, don't you ever wonder why I've never insisted you marry me? Why I've stood by and let you… just… *you know*… with other women?"

The hurt in her voice made me feel like the heel that I was. "I guess I've wondered. I'll marry you tomorrow, kitten. I'll marry you tonight. Say the word. Hell, I'll move us down to Florida and buy a fishing boat and we'll raise a passel of little Mikes and Veldas."

She flew out of my arms.

"What? Baby?"

Then she was standing in the middle of her little kitchen, her arms clutching herself in a desperate self-hug, sobbing, sobbing, from the tip of her toes to the top of her head. Such a tall woman, now she looked small, petite. Tiny in her sorrow.

I went up behind her and stood close, my hands on her shoulders.

"Kitten… what is it?"

"They tortured us, Mike. When they first had us. They tortured Civic and he told them everything he knew. They thought the two of us were partners, the way you and I are partners, and… but I didn't know the secrets that Civic did. I had nothing to tell them. They… they brought in a man that we later learned was the K.G.B.'s top expert in torture. He… he did terrible things to me, Mike. He did things to me with tools, with knives, with red-hot instruments of… of torture, Mike. *Inside* me, Mike. He…"

She was sobbing again, her body wracked with shuddering sobs.

"Baby… baby… don't put yourself through it."

I heard her swallow. She turned to me. She looked so small without her heels, in bare feet, just a frightened little girl.

"Okay, Mike… I'll say nothing more about that. Well, there's *one* other thing to say, but…"

"Honey. Please don't…"

Her smile was a terrible crooked thing. "Mike, when we first met… when I was on that undercover assignment with the Vice Squad, that horrible man I was working to put away… I… I had to get close to him. Surely you knew that."

Why was she jumping to this subject?

"Sure," I said, "of course, you'd have to get close to him."

I hadn't known she was working Vice back them—I thought she was just a poor kid victimized by a sadist. Which was why I killed the slob.

"And later, Mike, you knew I'd been in the O.S.S., and… well, from the first time I met you, you had this *thing* about wanting the woman you married to be a virgin. It was… so cute. So sweet. So old-fashioned. So… unrealistic. Mike, I lied to you. All those years. Why you believed me, I'll never know."

"Not important, kitten. Not important."

She sat at the kitchen table. Folded her hands as if saying grace. She was staring into nothing. I sat beside her, put a hand on her shoulder.

She said, "You're such a big dumb lug. I could tell you I lost it riding my bike, and you'd buy it. So you wanted to marry a virgin. I'd be a virgin for you. But it was a lie."

"I don't care, Vel. I don't care."

Now she turned her lovely face to me, streaked with tears and snot and desperation. "What that beast did to me in Russia, Mike…" She beat her belly with a small fist. "The doctors… over there… later… the doctors… here. Mike, there can't ever be any little Mikes and Veldas. That Commie bastard stole them from us, Mike. He… he… *stole* them from us…"

And she fell into my arms and I carried her back to the couch and held her in my arms cradled like a child. She wept. And then she slept. Not long.

Just long enough for me to imagine a million ways I would torture that torturer if I ever got my hands on him. But the impossibility of that was a torture that I knew I would suffer for the rest of my life…

Finally, Velda got up and went into the bathroom a while. I heard the water in the bathroom basin running. She returned in the same terrycloth robe, but she'd redone her make-up and she looked fresh and new. Across from where we sat was a gas fireplace and she got that going, switching off the end table lamp that had been the only other light in the room, to let the flames flicker orange and blue against the darkness. As the fire reflections lashed her flesh, she moved cat-like over to her stereo console and let the soft strains of Tchaikovsky's *Pathétique* fill the room.

Then she came and sat beside me again. The smell of her was a subtle, heady thing, nothing but soap and the natural scent of her, and I closed my eyes with the sheer pleasure of being close to her.

Velda let out a soft moan as her mouth reached for mine. The kiss had a liquid warmth sparked by the fire of her tongue that spoke of all the longing she had known these past months too, and all the secret hurt of so many years. The robe slipped off as if of its own accord, and her skin was pure velvet under my hands, every vital curve and hollow of her trembling with desire. My fingers drifted across the tips of her breasts, bringing them to instant rigidity. When I gently touched her stomach I could feel the concave plane of it flex with the knowledge that there were other places to explore and she squirmed with a feline movement to give me access to all of her.

Then she slipped from my arms and stood before me, loomed above me, tall again suddenly, a goddess with a mane of black, uncombed hair, gypsy wild, high full breasts and a narrow waist and flaring hips and more wild dark curls. She gave me a wicked smile. She crooked a finger, like a mother summoning a naughty child.

On the round braid carpet in front of the fire, she got down on all fours, then looked over her shoulder at me, as the twin globes of flesh beckoned, and she said, "Take me, Mike. Take me where I *am* a virgin... Take me... *Take* me..."

I took her.

The record ended, but we never noticed. The music we made ourselves was wilder and louder, the theme of it bigger than any instrument could interpret, ending in a smashing climax that seemed to wipe out time itself, the present, and the past.

CHAPTER TEN

The sky still had its gray lid over the pressure cooker of New York, holding in not heat but cold, a clammy cold, unsure of whether it wanted to rain or snow. The sidewalk crowds moved in hunched-over lockstep, raincoats clutched at throats, men's trouser legs flapping like flags, women holding down their skirts, even those in minis.

I liked this weather. The chill helped me think. It kept me alert, thanks in part to various old wounds including the shot in my leg that had started this all. Old wounds could help you prevent new ones, if you paid attention and weren't reckless. Of course, sometimes the latter could be a problem for me.

The Trib Building was old-fashioned enough to still use elevator operators. I got off on the familiar floor and didn't bother knocking at the door with the gold letters that said HY GARDNER. There was no reception area, the office big enough to accommodate both Hy at his big desk across the room and the bouffant blonde he used as a secretary at her desk where you came in.

She was very efficient and not there for her considerable good looks, since Hy's wife Marilyn, a former secretary of his herself, wouldn't have put up with that. Still, the peroxide had apparently damaged certain brain cells, as when I told her to go out for a smoke, she just showed me the big blue eyes and said, "You know I don't smoke, Mr. Hammer."

I jerked a thumb at the door. "Start."

When she was gone, I pulled up the visitor's chair and tossed my hat on Hy's desk, while he swung around from his typewriter on its stand.

"You always have had a way with the ladies, Mike." He was smiling that knowing little grin.

"Knowing" was right—a top columnist like Hy knew where just about every body was buried. If you saw this modest-sized man with his unremarkable pan, just a pair of glasses and a receding hairline and a born snooper's droopy nose, you would never know the power he wielded.

I watched him light up one of his ever-present cigars. It smelled like Havana in there, but in a good way.

He waved out his match and said, "That M.P. you got assigned to you seems like a bright fella. Also looks like he could bench-press a Cadillac."

"He's the real goods, Hy. You know why I'm here. You may have thought Des was bright, but there were still things you didn't want to tell him. You wanted me here in person. Here I am."

"Lucky me." His glasses had slid down his nose and he was looking over them. "Mike, you do understand there's a kind of unwritten agreement between the press and the politicians."

"Do I?"

"We had a president a while back who couldn't keep it in his pants."

"That was the rumor."

"But it didn't get in the papers, or on the radio, or on the TV."

"Oh. *That* unwritten agreement."

Hy nodded, rocking back in his leather desk chair. Behind him were metal filing cabinets. On the side walls were enough pictures of him with famous celebrities and politicians to rival those in Senator Jasper's office.

"So you are or aren't going to tell me?" I asked. "Or do I have to read between the lines?"

"They wouldn't be that hard to read between, kid."

"Spare me the trouble anyway, Hy. Or do you think I'm a security risk?"

His smile was small but it was the guardian of big secrets. "Mike, I like Allen Jasper. We need more like him. I like his brand of politics. He sits on powerful committees, and he doesn't try the grandstanding bull that brought McCarthy down. And he can't be bought."

"Can he be blackmailed?"

Hy put his cigar in a tray, leaving him wreathed with smoke. "I didn't say that."

"There's something in his private life that may be a weak spot. How's that for reading between the lines?"

Hy put his glasses back in place and leaned forward. He folded his hands on top of the news copy he'd been checking.

"Mike, the senator has a lovely wife. Wonderful wife, and children, really just the kind of ideal American family that helps keep a politico in office. Allen Jasper could have a shot at the White House one of these days, if he plays his cards right."

"But is he? Playing his cards right?"

Hy shrugged, retrieved his cigar and puffed at it, sending up smoke signals I could just about read.

"I met Emily Jasper myself," I said. "When you say she's lovely and she's wonderful, I agree. But she's also overweight, thanks to bearing the senator his lovely, wonderful children and because middle age is an unforgiving bastard."

"You're getting warmer, Mike."

"I spent enough time with Allen to know he has an eye for a well-turned calf. He never did anything out of line on that trip— too much of a pro for that—but he made remarks. And when I got friendly with the little gal the Russians provided to translate for us, he could have rightly had a shit fit. Man, was that a breech of protocol."

"So if I told you," Hy said, "way off the record, that he has a history of extra-marital activities, you wouldn't fall off that chair and sue me."

"No. I think he should be punched in the face for cheating on that great wife of his, but no."

"Mike, people who screw in glass houses shouldn't cast stones."

I batted the air. "Last time I looked, I wasn't married and I wasn't a United States senator. If he's playing around, he's an idiot a bunch of ways."

"I can't argue with you," Hy said with a shrug. "And things are changing. Look at the Profumo affair and how the British press blew it wide open."

"This is why I hate politics," I said. "Even the good ones are sons of bitches. Listen, Des showed you the list of guests at Jasper's party. Anybody there I should be talking to?"

Hy shook his head. "The only one involved in top-secret projects is Dr. Giles, and he's at least semi-retired. Maybe that Contreaux chick who works for him is worth a chat. Yeah, Mike, definitely you should talk to her. Tell her your theories about how a guy should be faithful to his best gal. How *is* Velda, by the way?"

I grinned at him. "Screw you, buddy. You know anything about those top-secret projects?"

"No. Just that Giles has been tied in with N.A.S.A. since the start. Other than that, it's outside my area. N.A.S.A. scientists almost never star in Broadway plays."

"Suppose not." I shifted in the chair. "You ever hear of something called Complex 90?"

"No. What is it, a new vitamin pill?"

"Maybe one of those top-secret projects you mentioned." I told him about the death of Lisa Contreaux's science-nerd boyfriend.

"Maybe you really should talk to that doll," Hy said.

"Anybody else on that list I should check up on? What about that Wall Street whiz, Warren Bentley?"

Hy shook his head. "Don't bother. Strictly high finance stuff. Nothing government-related."

"Well, if it's not breeching the security of the *Trib*'s top columnist, is this Bentley character really going to marry Irene Carroll?"

Hy laughed and choked on a bushel of cigar smoke doing it. I waited for him not to die, and finally he said, "Are you kidding? Have you met the guy?"

"I saw him at Jasper's party. I only talked to a handful of the guests and he wasn't one of them. I was just doing my security job."

Still chuckling, Hy shook his hand sideways. "The guy's a fly ball, Mike. Irene Carroll's strictly his beard."

"No kidding. So *that's* a secret, too. You must have an unwritten agreement with that crowd, too."

"Actually, we do. That, as we say, is showbiz. Don't be a prude, Mike. Irene Carroll helping out a nice guy like Bentley doesn't hurt anybody."

"I didn't say it did. But it does raise an interesting question."

"Yeah?"

I got up, stuffed on my hat. "What's in it for Irene Carroll?"

I had been to this townhouse before, on the night of the party when Lisa Contreaux, Dr. Giles, and I had grabbed a cab that brought us here, for the doc to patch me up. Just off Fifth Avenue, opposite Central Park, it was a newly restored three-story brownstone that on the first floor housed the doctor's exclusive practice. I vaguely remembered him mentioning that night that he lived in an apartment above.

From a booth in the Trib Building's lobby, I had called Lisa Contreaux and found her at home, and willing to talk. She'd given me an address.

This address.

I walked up the stairs to the landing where her apartment took up the entire third floor. I buzzed, and she answered, smiling in a very friendly way, immediately rekindling the rapport we'd had months ago at that ill-fated party.

Liz Taylor's imaginary sister had been under-dressed at that cocktail party, wearing a light blue satin blouse and a navy pencil skirt. Now months later, by odd coincidence, she'd selected the same outfit, making her over-dressed in this context. And she had on something else that she'd worn that night, too: Evening in Paris perfume.

"I was just about to give up on you," she said, holding the door open.

She was a doll, all right. Her heavily lashed big brown eyes with those dark, unplucked eyebrows and that bright red-lipsticked mouth provided a stark contrast with her ghostly pale complexion. The beauty mark near her mouth gave her glamour, and the black Carmen-like curls reminded me of the way Velda's hair had not long ago dried into a gypsy tousle.

The thought of Velda, and the pact we'd made last night, would have to guide me through the questioning of this beauty.

People in glass houses, as Hy had said…

After moving through a small entryway, we were in a large living room with a nice window onto the park, but the furnishings were unremarkable in an anonymously contemporary way, the colors muted, pastel. A few nice framed prints were spotted here and there, including a large one over the white-plaster fireplace, impressionistic Parisian scenes, maybe to go with the perfume.

She took my trenchcoat and hat and laid them carefully on a

chair. Then she closed the curtains over the picture window on the park, as if she thought the trees might eavesdrop. Only one light was on, a subdued yellow-glow lamp by the couch. On this overcast morning, no light in particular found its way in, and it might have been midnight.

Taking my arm at the elbow, she led me to the couch. "Would you like something to drink? Coffee, perhaps? A soft drink? Beer?"

"It's a little early, but… beer would be fine."

"I'll join you."

She returned with two poured Pilsner glasses of dark liquid.

"I hope you like Guinness," she said, sitting on the couch beside me.

"Being of good Irish stock," I said, and sipped and savored, "it's a requirement."

I set the glass on a coaster on the blond coffee table before us.

"What did you want to see me about, Mike?"

Apparently we were on a first-name basis after our brief meeting at the Jasper party.

"A couple of things," I said. "By the way, my condolences. I understand your fiancé—Dennis? Was in a tragic accident recently."

She nodded, her expression turning somber. "Yes. He was a sweet boy, a brilliant boy."

"Did the cops ever track down the hit-and-run driver?"

"No. But I just know it was some callow undergraduate. I'm afraid Manheim University has a deserved reputation as a party school. Lots of drinking among the frat crowd. Reprehensible."

She said this as she sipped at her pre-noon glass of Guinness.

"We don't know each other very well, Lisa, but maybe you've heard I have a reputation for being blunt. Meaning no disrespect to the dead, I just can't see a beautiful woman like you getting next to a gawky kid like that."

She bristled. "Mike—there *are* women who are looking for more out of a man than just a nice set of broad shoulders. Dennis was a genius, or nearly so. He worked closely with Dr. Giles, and was on his way to the top of his field. His... social graces may have been lacking, but he was a fine young man."

"Hey, I've been told my social graces are lacking."

That got a smile out of her, and there was nothing bristling in her tone when she said, "I have no prejudice against muscles, Mike. But I have a feeling you're more than just brawn yourself. A detective of your... caliber? Could hardly have achieved that status without considerable mental prowess."

"Maybe. But my caliber is .45, and hanging around with a gal who's got a PhD in physics could give a guy an inferiority complex."

She smiled and her tongue darted over the red lips, making them glisten wetly. She squeezed my shoulder, with a nice familiarity before withdrawing it. "Mike, you have nothing to worry about."

"Speaking of complexes, what do you make of Dennis's last words? 'Complex 90'? Does that mean anything to you?"

The unplucked eyebrows traveled higher. "Actually, it does. It's the project that he and Dr. Giles were working on together. But I'm afraid the nature of it is strictly classified by the government."

Having official credentials has its benefits. I got out the fancy blue-and-gold I.D. card with the embossed seal of Rickerby's group and let her take a gander.

"I'm not here strictly as a private eye," I said, putting the I.D. away, "or a private citizen. I'm investigating the circumstances of the party Senator Jasper threw."

She frowned in confusion. "Why would that event need investigating, Mike?"

"We think it started a spiral of events the culmination of which hasn't yet been reached. Possibly I interrupted an assassination attempt on the senator."

"You really think so? As I understood it, that Carroll's woman's jewelry is what that creature was after."

"The Carroll dame wasn't even there yet, but of course maybe our party-crasher didn't know that. I saw him, no doubt about it, make a beeline for the senator. Also, this 'creature'—his name was Pietro Romanos—was a championship shooter. A crack shot. That's the makings of an assassin, doll."

She didn't seem to mind being called "doll" by me. I admit I was testing the waters.

When she shrugged, the full breasts under the rather tight satin bobbed distractingly. "All right, Mike. Granted that party, and possibly those attending, are worthy of investigation. But what does that have to do with Dennis's tragedy?"

"Dennis was one of the partygoers. And now he's dead. Hit-and-run is a longstanding, time-honored method of covering up a murder even as it's being committed."

Those great big brown eyes got even bigger. "Dennis… murdered? Why?"

"I have no idea. But his last words may point us in the right direction. Which brings us back to 'Complex 90,' Lisa. What is it?"

She thought for a while, hands folded in her lap like a wallflower clutching a corsage, hoping to get a dance. I leaned back and sipped Guinness and waited for her decision.

Finally, she said, "Complex 90, putting it simply, is an organic formula that protects astronauts from space viruses."

Giles had said something on the subject at the party. It had, of course, gone over my head. Right into Outer Space.

"I didn't even know viruses could exist beyond the atmosphere," I said.

"Bacteria can travel, but that is only part of the problem. A latent virus can reactivate on a space flight, something as minor as a cold sore erupting into a life-threatening problem for an astronaut. There is also a theory that assorted influenzas that have hit hard in various countries have entered our atmosphere via cosmic dust and micro-meteorites."

"And this Complex 90 is a kind of... inoculation against space viruses?"

"It would be or *could* be, if Dr. Giles is successful in developing it. From everything I understand, despite several breakthroughs, he's years away."

"But tell me this, Lisa. Suppose he'd found it, the answer, the cure. Or even just had research pointing in the right direction. Is that something the Soviets might want?"

She laughed and the red smile was wide and lush. "Oh, yes. My goodness, yes. Whoever has this formula will be way, way ahead in the space race. We would vault into a first position the

Russians could only dream of attaining."

I thought about that. Then I asked, "But why would 'Complex 90' be the Dorfman kid's last words?"

She shrugged and her expression was weary and frustrated. "At first, I spent hours thinking about that very thing, wondering if perhaps he'd made a breakthrough and wanted to make sure we knew."

"Had he?"

"No, not according to Dr. Giles. But I finally came to understand, or at least I came to hold a belief that I find... comforting."

"Okay. What is it?"

"Dennis was unconscious at the accident scene, the ambulance attendants said, but then came around when they were loading him in, but was in a delirious state. The project had been so important to him, those words were a natural thing to come to his lips. I think, I really *believe*, that he knew he was in trouble, even knew he was dying, and the importance of the project he was being forced to abandon sprang to his consciousness."

That was a pretty long-winded way of saying, "Because it was important to him," but maybe when you were under thirty and had a doctorate in physics you had a right to be windy.

"Mike... do you really think Dennis was murdered?"

"It's a possibility."

"Are you looking into it? *Would* you look into it? For me? If it doesn't fall under the umbrella of this government investigation you're conducting, I could hire you as a *private* investigator. That's what you are, isn't it?"

"It's what I am."

"I make a decent salary. What kind of retainer would you need?"

"Nothing. I've already decided to look into Dorfman's death, whether it's part of the federal inquiry or not."

She closed her eyes and her smile was one of relief, but there was sorrow in it, too. When she opened those eyes again, they were glistening. "Thank you. Thank you, Mike. Dennis didn't deserve to die like that. So young. So brilliant."

Everything she said about him screamed respect, but nothing murmured passion.

I gestured around the place. "I didn't know you lived above Dr. Giles. Does he own this townhouse?"

She nodded. "I'm very lucky. It's a little extra that comes with my job. He likes having me handy. Really facilitates the work, whether it's here or when we ride together out to the university."

"Can I be blunt again?"

"Certainly, Mike."

"Is your arrangement strictly business?"

"What do you mean… oh!" She laughed. "No, Mike, no, there's no personal relationship between the doctor and myself. We've become good friends, but it's, as you say, strictly business. Or in our case, strictly science. Why do you ask?"

"I'm a snoop."

She cocked her head, regarding me like something on a slide under her microscope. That lush, red mouth angled in a sly smile. "You certainly have a lot of questions about my personal life, don't you? Wondering about me and Dennis. Now about me and Dr. Giles. How does this factor into your investigation, Mike?"

"No reason. Just gathering information."

"Are you sure?"

She leaned in and that mouth melted over mine, and she found my hand and guided it to a satin-covered breast where I could feel the hardening of her nipple as it tried to burst through the smooth cloth. Then she found my other hand and guided it up under the skirt, moving it up to where her panties should be but instead I felt the pleasant harshness of forbidden curls. The kiss continued, and her tongue probed my mouth, like another scientific experiment she was conducting, and under my hands in those two intimate places, her body tightened and moved spasmodically, an invitation that became a demand.

Her hand was on me, too, and as her fingers scrambled like playful kittens after my zipper, and her mouth drew away for a breath, I said, "Lisa... sweetheart... no. Not right now."

She reared back, damn near startled. Her voice became husky, nothing of the no-nonsense scientist in it.

"No? Don't you want me? I wanted you the moment I saw you at Jasper's, Mike." Those big brown eyes got sleepy. "You were right about me. I need a man. A real man. Sweet as Dennis was, he was a boy. Show me what I've been missing, Mike... *show* me..."

"Not the right time, baby," I said, and I gave her a quick kiss, and got to my feet. She looked up at me, a beautiful mess. The Carmen hair was a mad tumble framing a face where that mouth was a sensuous smear of lipstick, and her skirt was hiked high enough to offer a glimpse of paradise. Her top two buttons had popped undone, and the braless breasts were heaving.

"You don't *want* to go, do you, Mike?" she laughed, and a hand of hers gripped me through my trousers, grabbing the part of me that wanted to stay.

"Lisa," I said, "that's the best retainer I've been offered in ages, but we'll have to take this up *later*."

I jammed my hat on and grabbed my trenchcoat, and she did not show me to the door. She stayed there on the couch, laughing at me in a way that seemed not at all intellectual.

On the way down the stairs, I used a handkerchief to wipe off the lipstick. I would have to remember to toss that damn hanky in a BEAUTIFY NEW YORK bin. If Velda found it, there'd be hell to pay.

Glass houses was right.

At the Blue Ribbon Restaurant on Forty-fourth, I sat at my corner table in the bar nursing a Four Roses and ginger, waiting half an hour for Des Casey to meet me, as we'd arranged. Then I asked for a phone and Angie brought one over. I tried my apartment number, where I thought Casey might be.

No answer.

I called Velda, who had stayed home for the morning, waiting until I came up with a new assignment for her. She had heard from Casey mid-morning.

"Des said he connected with an old cellmate pal of this Romanos character," she told me. "Apparently the week of the Jasper party, Romanos was bragging about a big job he had coming up. Something that would change everything for him."

"That could be a jewelry heist."

"I don't think so. I didn't give that to you exactly right, Mike. It was a '*big-paying* job.' And there's one other interesting wrinkle— Romanos told his pal he'd be out of touch for a while. Not just laying low—out of the country."

"A guy doesn't have to leave the country after a jewel heist."

"Not usually. You've lost track of your M.P.?"

"Yeah, Des was supposed to meet me at the Ribbon over half an hour ago."

"Well, you know traffic in this town."

"Vel, where was he calling you from? Did he say?"

"I think he was right here in the building. In your apartment. Should I go down and check?"

"No. Stay put. You'll hear from me."

We said goodbye and I hung up. I went out the back way, cut over to Broadway and caught a cab. Nobody seemed to be following. If that was bad guys who'd lost my trail, that was fine. If I'd shaken the good guys, maybe not so fine...

I could have said something to the agent posing as a doorman or the agent playing porter in the lobby, but I didn't. I just got on the elevator. When the doors closed, I pressed 9, then slid the .45 out of the sling, thumbed off the safety and full-cocked the hammer back.

I tucked myself by the front right corner of the elevator car and when the doors opened, I was ready. But nothing happened. I edged out into the hall and made my way down to 9-E. Carefully, as close to silent as humanly possible, I got to my door, and listened.

Nothing.

Just silence, but that funny kind of silence that wasn't silence at all, because city sounds were mixed in and building noise and then the soft speech of two men exchanging a few words, not outside, not elsewhere in the building, but right inside my apartment, not far beyond that door, just some friendly, small conversation.

In Russian.

I didn't use my key. I used my foot, which was risky, because kicking open doors isn't as easy in real life as it is in the movies and on TV, and if I didn't hit just the right spot with just the right force, I would be announcing myself and bullets could come punching through the wood of that door into me, ending this before it began, getting me out of the game before I even the knew players.

I kicked it just right.

It flew off its hinges and I flew into the darkened apartment, no lights on in my little living room, the blinds onto the street shut, but the hallway light exposed them, all three of them, the smaller one in the topcoat and the big man in the raincoat and the M.P. in civvies on the floor, sprawled there, possibly dead, certainly unconscious, his face to one side in a pool of blood from his nose and mouth.

The prone Des Casey was between us but the smaller of the two—a man said to be a master of disguise, though in the muted light the shape of him was the same—was my visitor from the office, aka Soviet assassin Felipe Mandau, who was digging in his topcoat pocket for his weapon when my .45 slug caught him in the shoulder and knocked him back on his ass. The other guy, a big bald guy deeper in the living room near the window with the blinds, was just a monstrous silhouette, but he already had his gun out, and it blasted orange flame at me, the bullet going way high as I dropped to the floor, near where Casey lay—*breathing, I could see him breathing!*—and when I came up with the .45 ready to return fire, the big guy threw a lamp at me, catching my shoulder, and the .45 sprung out of my grasp as I saw him lumbering toward me. I scrambled to my feet just in time for him to grab me by the trenchcoat lapels and toss me like a shot put into my couch, sending it over on its back and me with it, ass over teakettle. Then he was looming over me, just a black shape, and the barrel of his Makarov was pointing down at me.

"Do not move, Hammer," a thickly Russian-accented voice ordered. The guy was six two, easy.

I was on my back on the overturned couch, and that put my feet in a perfect position to kick him, and both feet caught him in the chest and he went back, smacking into a cabinet, the Makarov flying. I threw myself at him, taking him the rest of the way down, and I slammed my fists into him, his face, his chest, his breadbasket, but nothing seemed to have much effect. The big man scrambled backward under me, grasping at anything, and that was when he grabbed the blinds and pulled them down just as sun was finding its way through the clouds to send a laser beam of light into my face…

…through the scarred-edged quarter-size hole in the middle of the big man's right palm.

The hole that I had made with a ball-peen hammer when I slammed a twenty-penny nail into his hand into the floor of that barn.

The face looking up at me, with big yellow teeth bared under a thick mustache, his cheekbones Apache high, nostrils flared in the Slavic face, belonged to an assassin named Gorlin. Code name: *the Dragon.* The surviving half, anyway.

I was straddling the son of a bitch now, my knees on his shoulders, pinning him down, a great big man like a little bug on its back, wriggling, squirming, but I just hunkered over him and laughed in his face, my spittle flecking his high cheekbones like tiny tears, my hands digging in around his throat and I squeezed and squeezed and savored the way his eyes popped out and how his tongue lolled like a thirsty dog's.

I had damn near finished the fucker when an arm looped around my neck and yanked me backward and I turned my head just enough to see Mandau, his eyes popping there, too, but not the way the Dragon's had been, his smaller yellow teeth exposed in an awful smile, and his free hand with a hypodermic needle in it was seeking the exposed flesh of the side of my neck.

Mandau hadn't been going for a weapon, at least not a gun: it was a needle! They *did* want to abduct me again, that's why the Dragon hadn't shot me when he had the chance, and my hands were off Gorlin's throat and reaching around to try to get at my hypo-wielding attacker when the Dragon grabbed me by the wrists and held me there, that needle in his comrade's grasp maybe an eighth of an inch from my throat when something, somebody, ripped the smaller man off the back of me like a scab.

Des Casey, his face bloody, looking as dazed as a drunk, which meant he was likely badly concussed, had hauled the little man with the big needle off me and I was still smiling like a lunatic when the Dragon was on me, flinging me aside again, and I bumped hard against the underside of the couch, hard enough to knock the wind out of me, so that I was just half-sitting, half-standing there when the Dragon, who had found his gun, shot Des Casey in the head.

The M.P.'s eyes emptied of life and that once strong body fell like a stringless marionette to the floor and I saw my .45, dove for my .45, and it was in my hand as the two Russians ran pell mell from the apartment, my slugs raining their way, chewing up walls and furniture and making thunder in the small room, taking Mandau's head apart in red jagged chunks, but the Dragon was out the door, and by the time I got to my feet and pursued, navigating the dead, I slipped in somebody's blood and knocked my head into the side of a table. It stunned me just enough to slow me, and when I got into the hall, it was empty, other than the billowing curtains down at the other end where the window on the fire escape was up.

I ran there, leaned out with my rod ready but saw no one on the metal stairs and wondered if I'd been suckered, that maybe Gorlin had taken some other escape route. I went to check the elevator just as Velda stepped off, wide-eyed and ready with a .32 Browning in her hand. She had heard the shots from two floors down and come up to help.

But when we went back to check Des Casey, there was no helping him.

The M.P. was dead.

"He's back, Velda," I said.

"What? Who?"

"The Dragon. Comrade Gorlin. Rickerby lied to me—and I will know the goddamn reason why!"

That was when a brace of Rickerby's agents, those faithful watchdogs from across the street and down in the lobby, came racing up to our rescue.

"Just in the nick of time, boys," I told them.

CHAPTER ELEVEN

In the conference room at Peerage Brokers, I again sat at the big oblong table. Narrow-faced Vincent Worth of Special Sections, in another three-piece suit, played *paterfamilias* at its head. That gray little fed Art Rickerby again stood at the window, with his back to us, and Tony Wale sat opposite me with a wary expression, maybe afraid I'd drag his ass across the table again.

Not a word had yet been said, though I'd come in a good two minutes ago. It was like hot-rodding kids playing a game of chicken, and whoever went off the line first might drive off the cliff. But I was going to make them go first. I was curious to see just how stupid these feds could be.

Rickerby couldn't look at me. He pretended to be studying what was left of the overcast afternoon, separating two slats of the blinds to do so. But I knew he couldn't meet my gaze. My buddy Art. My pal Art. My betrayer Art.

The aftermath of the melee in my apartment might have taken the rest of the day sorting out, but it didn't. That's where it comes in handy having an NYPD Captain of Homicide for a best friend. Shortly after several of the federal watchdogs had come rushing belatedly to my defense, two uniformed beat officers were on their heels. Just for the entertainment value, I stood by listening to them argue jurisdiction for maybe five minutes, then told the older of the uniformed pair to call Pat Chambers.

Within an hour, Pat had worked things out with one of Rickerby's people, and I had given a detailed statement. The crime scene and whatever follow-up was necessary would be handled jointly by the Homicide Bureau and the local F.B.I. office. Everybody was happy, except maybe the late Felipe Mandau.

And me.

"Mr. Hammer," Worth said finally, "this incident changes everything. It will be almost impossible to keep this out of the press. And if it's known we're allowing you to traipse around the city getting into shoot-outs and creating general mayhem, we will be rightly accused of reckless endangerment of the public."

I said nothing.

Worth's frozen gray eyes remained fixed on me. "That leaves us with only two viable options. One, that you go into immediate protective custody at a military base, and I would suggest that Miss Sterling accompany you, to prevent her from being used as leverage against you. This, obviously, would be the most prudent option."

I said nothing.

"Two," Worth continued, "we step up our protective measures, even as we appear to back off—giving the impression that we have thrown our hands in the air and left you to your own devices. In reality, you would be virtually surrounded by our people."

I said nothing.

Tony Wale, gingerly, said, "Mike, this is the option we encouraged you to accept at our last meeting. We use you as bait to attract the remaining Soviet agents. But then we are right there to swoop in."

That was when I began to laugh. A good old-fashioned horse laugh that stopped just short of tears, though there was plenty to cry about.

"When your people 'swooped in,' today," I said, "the party was so long over, the street-cleaners were sweeping up the confetti. No. No more shadowing me and Velda, no more agents watching us from across the street or from the lobby of my apartment building or down the hall from my office. Pull everybody off. Now. Right now."

Worth tried out a small smile on that narrow, somber face; it didn't play well. "All right, then. Option number one. We'll get you and Miss Sterling cleared out this afternoon and on a plane to—"

"No protective custody, either," I said. "I'm just a private citizen, going about his business."

Worth was shaking his head. "Unacceptable, Hammer."

"Mister" had gone the way of all flesh.

I said, "I'm not going into some kind of protective custody, like the witness in a damn mob trial... remember that Murder Inc. clown who got tossed out a window at Coney Island, in protective custody? And anyway, if I did allow that, how do I know my next stop isn't the Soviet Union, thanks to some extradition deal that the politicians cook up?"

Worth didn't deny it.

I said, "I need to find you fellas a real live K.G.B. agent that I can trade you for getting my life back. And the only way I can do that is on my own."

Wale said, "Mike, you can't stop us from putting men out in the field to protect you."

"I am going to assume anybody tailing me is the enemy. I am going to assume anybody watching me is the enemy. You may have noticed how I handle enemies. I warned you people at the beginning of this damn thing."

Rickerby still had his back to us, looking out that window at a dark gray sky full of rain that refused to come down.

Worth said, "Are you threatening to kill federal agents, Mr. Hammer?"

"No. I'm promising to defend myself. But before I put myself in that position, I'll have a press conference. Just like the politicians. I'll tell this city and this country and the whole wide world about how you are screwing up. How I was almost killed today under the watchful eye of dozens of federal agents."

Worth glanced at Tony Wale, who shrugged. Then Worth looked to Rickerby, whose back remained to us.

"All right," Worth sighed. "I believe the expression is… 'it's your funeral.' Now get the hell out of here, Hammer."

"No," I said.

Worth's cool evaporated and fire melted the frozen eyes. "*What* did you say?"

"Sorry. What I meant to say was *hell*, no. You and Tony take five. Smoke 'em if you got 'em, fellas. Art and me, we need a little talk between old friends."

Worth's slice of a face was reddening. He was on his feet, and leaning his hands on the table. "Goddamn you, Hammer, you do *not*—"

"Vince," Rickerby said quietly, still looking out the window, "leave Mike and me alone. For just a few minutes. We... *I*... owe him that much."

Worth seemed as confused as he was angry, while Wale—who knew me too well—was just fine with getting out of that room.

When the door slammed, thunder shook the sky like an over-done echo. Rain came down. Hard. Insistent. And right on cue.

I got up and walked over to Rickerby and watched the reflections on his face of water trails streaming down the window. His expression was emotionless, but the rain streaks cast onto it were like tears.

"I didn't tell them, Art," I said, "who the other assassin was. But I told your guy at the scene. He obviously told you."

Rickerby's nod was so slight it almost didn't register.

"Comrade Gorlin," I said. "The Dragon—the tooth part, anyway. Was Mandau the new nail? Or is that somebody else?"

Rickerby said nothing.

"He's carrying around a hole in his hand that I gave him," I said. "That's one small solace. Fun to know that every time he washes his hands, he thinks of me. *If* the slob ever washes his hands."

"Mike..."

"You lied to me, Art. Back in that barn, I spared Comrade Gorlin's life for you, handed him to you on a platter, because you said a quick kill wasn't good enough. You said he would rot in a cell waiting for the day when he would take the long walk to that oaken chair with the big switch."

Thunder cracked the sky; lightning flashed on Rickerby's solemn face.

"What about Richie Cole, Art? The agent who was like a son to you? You said you'd made promises over his body, the way I once made promises over the body of a guy who gave an arm for me in the Pacific. You said nothing would stop you from taking your revenge and you sought me out as the best man for the job of hunting down the son of a bitch you would see dead."

"I didn't lie to you, Mike."

"Didn't you?"

He turned to me and half of his face wore the reflected gray streaky raindrops. "I meant those things when I said them. But when I brought in the surviving half of the Dragon team, my superiors insisted he was just too important to waste on execution. It's the same situation you're in, Mike, right now—the need for you to bring us a living K.G.B. agent captured on American soil. A catch like that is worth something."

"You traded Gorlin for agents of ours."

"Yes. *Five* agents, Mike. Agents like my late colleague Richie Cole, who were languishing in the kind of prison that you managed to escape. I don't have the luxury of your emotionalism, Mike. I am, for better or worse, a bureaucrat. A servant of the state. And I have to make decisions in the cold hard reality of a world on the brink of nuclear destruction."

Some of the anger had bled out of me. *Didn't swapping a piece of garbage like Gorlin in order to free five of our boys make a hell of a trade?*

Actually, no.

"Art, you gave Gorlin back to them, you let the Dragon out of his cage, and now *another* Richie Cole is dead—his name was Des Casey, Art, and he was a soldier, a decorated war hero and he died trying to save my life. He has a family here in New York and a girl back in D.C., and assuming they've gotten the word by now, they are in hell and will be there a long, long time. So I will tell you right now, Art, that if I can bring you back a Commie agent alive, I will— just call me Frank Buck, buddy. But it *won't* be Comrade Gorlin."

Rickerby nodded. He risked touching my sleeve, and I flinched a little, but then let him guide me to the table. He nodded for me to sit and I did. He sat next to me and he put his hand on my arm. I left it there.

"I know you think I let you down," Rickerby said. "And maybe I did. In this kind of deadly work, you make judgment calls that cost lives. But I will do this much for you, Mike. I'm going to see to it you have your way. All the watchdogs will be called off."

"I appreciate that, Art."

"You may be thanking me for your own death, so I'll pass on saying, 'You're welcome.' As for Comrade Gorlin, I ask only one thing."

"Yeah?"

"Make it slow."

"No problem."

He reached inside his suit coat and withdrew a picture, a surveillance photo of a tall, thin man with sunken pockmarked cheeks, a sharp nose and hooded eyes behind black round-frame glasses. His hair was gray and cropped close to the skull. Actually, he looked like a damn skull.

"Colonel Toy," Rickerby said. "We have confirmed that he is in the United States. Very likely right here in Manhattan, supervising the mission that Gorlin and Mandau botched today."

I studied it and gave it back to him. As he tucked the photo away, I said, "And if I bag that bastard, it'll free some of ours?"

"Yes. Do that, and I can all but guarantee you that you and Velda can return to your normal life." He smiled a little. "Well, your kind of normal life."

"There's something I need to give you."

"Oh?"

I got out my wallet and removed the I.D. with the fancy embossed seal, which I tossed on the table before him, like a sullen waiter delivering the check.

"If this goes wrong," I said, "you won't want my body turning up with that in my pocket."

"Understood."

"And, anyway, I don't think we're going to be doing any more jobs together. After today, I'm strictly an Old School private eye. In future, do me a favor? Spare me the cloak-and-dagger bullshit."

"Understood. Mike…"

"Yeah?"

"I know we won't be working together, and I know we'll never be friends again, but… I'd like to shake your hand."

What the hell.

We shook hands.

He was standing at the window when I left, crying his rain-reflected tears.

* * *

Late afternoon, I met Velda at the bar at P.J. Moriarty's on Sixth and Fifty-second. The rain had let up, but you could feel in the air that more was coming.

Neither of us was hungry, but we shared a corned beef sandwich just for fuel. No beer. Coffee. Caffeine was my friend.

"I think we can wrap this up tonight," I told her.

The sky was growling out there.

"Am I sticking with you?" she asked.

"No, I have an assignment for you. One last assignment on this job, and a damn important one."

"Oh?"

"Yeah. My life may depend it. And yours."

"Oh. Okay." She nibbled at the edge of her half of the sandwich. "The *Dragon* back? It's crazy, Mike. Unreal."

"Oh, it's real all right."

"Funny." She shook her head. "To think, that Commie creep tracking me all the way back to the U.S., ready to kill me on sight… and yet I never ever saw the S.O.B. myself."

"It's often that way with the hunter and the hunted."

"Good thing you saw him first, Mike." She took another nibble, rolled those dark lovely eyes. "Hard to believe that Rickerby would let that monster go."

"Art was trying to save lives."

She touched my hand. "Mike… I'm sorry about Des. I know you really liked him. He was a good guy."

"Just a damn kid."

"No, he was older than that. He was a soldier. He went out the way he would have wanted."

"No, Velda. No soldier really wants to die in combat. Like Patton said, it's all about killing the other guy."

"Good point." She gave me a nasty, teasing smile as she prepared to take another nibble out of her half sandwich. "Gonna do some killing tonight, Mike?"

"Oh yeah."

"Forty-five more?"

"Not that many." I grinned at her. "I'm in a quality over quantity mood, doll. Pass that mustard, and I'll fill you in on your assignment."

I was in no mood to deal with the Wentworth Hotel's arcane system of monitoring those calling on their guests. I went in the employee entrance off the alley, moving through the kitchen like I knew what I was doing, and bribed a waiter to let me use the service elevator. No matter how posh the hotel, the ass end of it smells like a garbage truck. The Wentworth was no exception.

When I knocked at Irene Carroll's door, it took her a while to answer. Finally, I heard footsteps padding on the other side of the door, and I stepped to one side so she couldn't check the peephole. I figured she'd assume it was a hotel staffer, since that was the regular drill. And she did, opening the door, and I stepped inside, shutting it behind me.

She looked good, but maybe a little more of her age was showing than last time. Her nice full figure was swathed in a light blue quilted housecoat, its belt hastily tied, and her legs and feet were bare. No make-up but for lipstick, and her white, chin-cut hair looked tousled.

Her eyes widened with surprise, almost alarm. "Mike! You weren't announced."

"I don't like to stand on ceremony," I said, brushing by, walking on into the pop-art-decorated living room. An ashtray on the glass coffee table had two cigarettes going in it and a couple of drink glasses. I smiled to myself.

As before, I sat on the red chair and she sat opposite me on the blue sofa.

I crossed my legs. Got comfortable.

"Yes?" she said impatiently, leaning forward, hands clasped. "Why are you *here*, Mr. Hammer?"

"What happened to 'Mike'?"

"Why are you here, Mike?"

"Just wanted to ask you a question."

"Just one?"

"Probably just one, or maybe two. That night, a few months ago—why were you late to Jasper's party?"

She tried to sound off-hand. "I ran late. I don't have any servants in the city, and—"

"Oh, no servants in the city. That must be a hardship for you."

She reached for the black enamel box and got out a cigarette. She was about to light one of the dark gold-tipped numbers when I said, "You've already got one going, Irene. In fact, you've already got two going."

She swallowed nervously, then went ahead and lit the fresh cigarette.

"Doesn't take much of a detective," she said, her voice brittle, "to figure out that I'm entertaining a guest. Let's be frank. A male guest."

"Yeah, since one cig has lipstick and the other doesn't, that would have been my deduction."

"So if you don't mind, now that you can see that you're intruding, would you please go? I'll be glad to talk to you later. Perhaps tomorrow?"

Still just getting comfortable, I unbuttoned my suit coat, giving her a glimpse of the .45 in the sling under my left arm. "Answer my question, Irene, and I'll just toddle along."

She swallowed thickly. "As I say, I didn't go to the party until later because I was running late." She forced the trademark tinkly laugh. "I am *notorious* for arriving late, and—"

"You weren't avoiding the shooting that you knew would take place?"

She practically dropped the smoke, her eyes wide, her mouth an attractive trapdoor that had sprung. "No! I had no *idea*..."

I folded my arms. "There was another Washington hostess, probably your chief rival a few years ago... remember her? The wife of a senator. Want to hear something wild? She was a Russian spy, perfectly positioned to know not only what her powerful husband knew, but, in her charming way, to meet and gain the confidence of all sorts of persons in critical positions in our government and foreign ones. Strangely, a number of those persons died—some of natural causes, others violently, including her own husband during a break-in at their mansion upstate. Get this—an attempted jewel robbery. Small world, huh?"

"I knew that woman," Irene said. She had folded her arms, as well. "She was no spy. She died at her home in a terrible accident."

"Yeah, I know. I arranged it. You see, she was half of an assassination team—she teed the victims up, and the other half hit a hole in one. Like you said, she's gone. Dead. But the other half of that team is back. He tried to kill me today. Unsuccessfully, as you may have gathered. But he did manage to kill a nice young M.P. who was protecting me. So my question to you, Irene, is… are you the replacement for that other Washington hostess?"

"*That's enough!*" a familiar male voice shouted from a hallway.

Senator Allen Jasper entered in a dark-colored robe of his own that indicated just how frequently he spent time at Irene Carroll's pad.

Angry as hell, Jasper stood with the crying comic-book woman on the wall just behind him, as if she were the one he was defending as he said, "Irene a spy? Are you out of your mind, man? Mike, get out of here. Now! You've gone completely around the bend."

I gestured easily, smiling like the old friend I was. "Sit down, Allen. I *thought* that might bring you out of your shell. By the way, you were casting a shadow where you were standing, eavesdropping. Cheating husbands need better skills than that."

He was breathing hard. She reached up a hand to him, touched the elbow of his robe, and he gazed down at her, swallowed, nodded, and sat beside her.

"You don't believe that nonsense you were spouting," Jasper said, much more quietly. "Irene a Russian spy? You can't mean that."

"Well, it's a workable theory. I've been considering it. And if

Irene *is* in the employ of the K.G.B., it would explain a lot… and like that other hostess, she's gotten close enough to you, Allen, to know exactly what you're doing and thinking."

He slipped an arm around her and she moved closer him, trembling. "This is nonsense, Mike," he said. "All right, you've found out our secret. We're having an affair, and we have been for some time. Satisfied?"

"Not really, but I'd imagine *you* are, frequently. Very convenient, living in the same building, you two. Irene, you were late that night because you were reluctant to be in the same room as Allen's wife—you remember Allen's wife, don't you? Emily? You told me how wonderful she was."

She was sniffling. "You're… you're cruel."

"Well, maybe it's because my ego got bruised, knowing that you coming on to me yesterday was just to make me think you were unattached. The way you use that Warren Bentley character as your beard."

Jasper was frowning at me, as hurt as he was angry. "Why are you doing this, Mike?"

I ignored the question. "Now I know why Ralph Marley wanted to quit his easy, high-paying easy gig with you, Allen—he didn't like being the guy who helped you sneak around on your wife. Marley was a straight shooter, a family man who loved his wife, and it rubbed him the wrong way."

"What is the *point* of this, Mike?"

"You've been lucky, you crazy kids, keeping your secret. The press has looked the other way. Hell, maybe your wife looks the other way, too, but I doubt it. She's probably like the rest of your constituents, who buy you as the upstanding guy you pretend to be."

Now Jasper's anger was gone and only the hurt remained. "Why are you doing this, Mike? What are you trying to prove?"

"Look, I'm no choir boy," I said. "Generally the only bedroom activities that interest me are my own. But you have a secret that can be used against you, Allen. Times are changing. The press may not always keep the lid on. Does the name Christine Keeler mean anything to you?"

He was shaking his head and she was trying to disappear into him. "Mike," he said desperately, "what are you after? What do you want?"

"The K.G.B. wanted me to take a trip to Russia. I think I know why, but even if the point was just to get revenge on me for past sins, I want to know how I came to be chosen as Ralph Marley's replacement."

He frowned in confusion. "Mike, *I* picked you. You were Marley's friend, helping out the night he got shot. But you'd done work for me before. You know that."

"You were the ideal blackmail target in this thing, Allen."

"No one blackmailed me in taking you along, Mike! No one!"

"No one pressured you to use me?"

"No. It was my choice."

That was not what I'd expected to hear.

"All right," I said, and I sat forward. I tried to take all of the threat out of my voice. "Think, and think carefully. Did anyone even suggest, in the most casual way, that I'd make a good replacement for Marley? Maybe the very night of the shooting?"

He thought about it, but only briefly. "Yes, Mike, there was someone. But it was, like you say, casual. Just conversation. Cocktail party conversation, at that."

"Who made this casual suggestion, Allen?"

And this time his response was exactly what I expected to hear.

The cab moved through the rain like a lumbering beast, but the sky was the greater beast, rumbling and roaring and flashing with incandescent fury, split by veins of electricity. It was coming down hard now, rain filling the gutters, machine-gunning umbrellas, sending even those New Yorkers made of the sternest stuff to seek shelter under marquees or to huddle in doorways or to cram inside bars that offered a more soothing kind of wet.

By the time I got dropped off, it had let up momentarily, as if God was grabbing a breath before His next expression of displeasure with the human race. The bottom floor of the townhouse, just off Fifth Avenue, opposite Central Park, bled light from its windows. I had expected to find that floor dark. At almost seven, there was no reason for a high-society, exclusive practice like that of Dr. Harmon Giles to be doing any business at all.

I had figured to get buzzed in and go up to the second floor landing of the doctor's apartment. I'd never been inside, but had passed it on my way up to visit Lisa Contreaux's top-floor pad yesterday.

But now I found myself knocking at the front office door. It was locked, of course, though the reception room was brightly lighted, if empty of patients, with no nurse or receptionist behind the counter across the room. I had just about given up, and was ready to return to my initial plan, when the doctor—in a white smock over dark trousers—peeked out from the hallway next to the receptionist's station. He squinted, trying to make me out through the rain-streaked glass.

"*Mike Hammer*, Doc!" I yelled. "Got a minute?"

He lifted his chin and smiled faintly in recognition and came across the room, unlocking the door. I stepped inside, only mildly damp. I'd spent most of the downpour in the cab.

"Glad I caught you, Doc," I said, and grinned. "I didn't figure you'd be open at this hour."

"Well, I'm not," he said, pleasant but not friendly, mildly put upon as he closed and re-locked the door behind me, "but I ran late today with some walk-ins."

I took the liberty of hanging up my wet trenchcoat and rain-sluiced hat on his metal rack.

He was saying, "I was just about to close up shop and go upstairs to my apartment. Is there something I can help you with, Mr. Hammer? I have appointment slots open for tomorrow. We can write something down…"

He was a somewhat bigger man than I remembered, but otherwise the same—in his mid-sixties with mustache, graying hair, wire-frame glasses, a distinguished variation on the old family doctor. He wasn't smoking his pipe, but the smell of tobacco was on him.

"It's this leg, Doc," I said, rubbing my thigh. "It's been giving me fits. Man, on a rainy day like this, it just screams at me."

"Well, it certainly shouldn't," he said. "That was a very simple procedure. We got the bullet out, and it seemed to be in one piece."

"Maybe you left behind a few fragments of shrapnel," I suggested. "Could you do something about it—now?"

He mulled that, sighed, and shrugged. "I suppose I can take a quick look at it."

"Would you mind, Doc?"

"Not at all." His smile was completely friendly now. "A good mechanic has to stand behind his work, right?"

"Yeah. I wouldn't want to break down in the middle of the Thruway."

He led me into and down the hallway and stopped at an open doorway, reached in, and switched the light on, illuminating a small, standard examining room. Nodding toward the elevated table with its crisp white tissue-paper covering, his back to me, he said, "Just remove your pants, Mr. Hammer, and have a seat. Be with you in a moment."

"Not in the mood to drop my drawers, Doc," I said, and he whirled and saw the .45 aimed his way. "Why don't you just hop up on that little table."

He did so, rather awkwardly. Now he knew how his patients felt. He was sitting there like a kid with his legs dangling and his expression was telling, because there was no confusion in it. Just fear.

"Tell me about Complex 90, Doc."

This did seem to surprise him. "Complex 90… Where did you hear *that* term?"

"Well, I wasn't there at the time, but those were the last words of a kid who used to assist you. Gawky, goofy-looking brain named Dennis Dorfman. Remember him?"

His face took on a sadness that was almost believable. "That was such a tragedy. Such a sad, premature end for so brilliant a young man."

"And yet somehow I think you're over it. Complex 90, Doc. Tell me about it."

Finally, his genial features hardened into a mask of contempt, and his eyes became as cold and unblinking as a stone statue's. "Why don't you tell me what you *think* you know, Mr. Hammer?"

"Well, I believe it's a formula, an organic formula I think was the phrase, to protect astronauts from space viruses, and from latent viruses they may have unknowingly brought with them into space."

His smile wasn't much of one. "Not bad for a layman, Mr. Hammer. But surely you know that Complex 90 is many years away from finalization. We are only in the initial stages."

"I don't think so. I think that's why Dennis Dorfman had to die. I believe he knew you'd had a breakthrough, and were hiding it. He may also have discovered your connections to a foreign government. That you'd sold the formula to them."

His mustache rode the sneer. "I didn't 'sell' anything to anyone."

"Oh. Then you're a good party member."

"I'm not a party member at all, Mr. Hammer. I'm a scientist in a very dangerous world, a world where the balance of weaponry and technology between two great superpowers must be maintained. Right now, America is in the lead in the space race."

"But with Complex 90, you figured to give the Russians a boost."

"Perhaps."

"So, then, you were planning to sell it to both sides?"

His eyes and nostrils flared. "There is no *sell* about it!"

"Why didn't you just defect, Doc? Or can you do more damage... I mean, 'good'... where you're currently placed? You can talk till you're *red* in the face... get it? ...but you'll never convince me you're not a Soviet agent. That you're just an idealist trying to maintain the balance of power."

The contempt was back. "And why is that, Mr. Hammer?"

"Because somebody close to Senator Jasper, somebody on the inside, had to stage-manage this rather elaborate farce. Somebody who had learned that I frequently worked for and with the senator's favorite bodyguard, Ralph Marley. Someone who knew that there were people in Moscow who would just love to get their hands on me, the guy behind the paint-factory massacre in '52, the guy who dismantled their top assassination team."

He was chuckling now. "You have an amazingly over-inflated opinion of your own value, Mr. Hammer."

"Maybe, but I was the perfect choice nonetheless. I was a guy who could serve his function and then be used for propaganda value. I was ideal for embarrassing the senator and the United States itself, by pinning an espionage rap on me. Even if it did cost the life of a nice Russian girl."

He was grinning now, eyes wide behind the wire-frames. "Are you listening to yourself, Mr. Hammer? Have you enough of a grip on reality to know how *ridiculous* this all sounds?"

"You were on the inside, Doc. You were a friend of Jasper's, someone he respected because of your N.A.S.A. work. You were close enough to know... whether as a trusted friend or just an observant bystander… that the senator and Irene Carroll were having an affair. That would be the ideal blackmail vehicle for getting the senator to agree to hire me as his bodyguard on the Russia junket."

"I did no such thing."

"No, you didn't. You didn't have to. Things had been put so perfectly into motion that Allen, as if he'd been brainwashed to do so, selected me as his Russian-trip bodyguard. No major prompting needed. All you did was gently suggest to Allen, after the shooting on the night of the party, that he was lucky to have me at the ready to step in for poor Ralph Marley."

He gestured with both hands. "I suggested you to him. And what of it?"

I gestured with the .45. "I know there are others in this with you. I doubt you could have reached out to Pietro Romanos for this job. Whoever thought to hire a sharp shooter to play jewel thief knows his stuff, that's for sure. Romanos could have easily shot the senator, no matter who pushed him aside. All you need is a head shot, a cinch for a champion shooter like Romanos. No, Romanos had two jobs to do the night of the party—shoot and kill Ralph Marley… and shoot me in the leg."

He was chuckling again. "Wounding you, I suppose, to make a hero of you, but not so badly as to keep you from taking Marley's place on the Russian trip? Simply absurd, Mr. Hammer. Ludicrous. Below even a man of your doggedly average intelligence."

"Nice try, Doc. No, that's not why Marley was to wound me, and specifically in muscle tissue, where some residual ache might be expected. No, this was about Complex 90. About smuggling it into the Russia in the most unexpected and frankly amusing way. And this is why no one has tried to kill me—why I'm still the target of abduction. Maybe you hope to have my ass hauled back to Russia, or possibly just want to make sure I'm not dead till you're through with me—so that there are no embarrassing discoveries during the autopsy."

Now he was afraid that I knew. And I did know. "What are you saying, Mr. Hammer?"

"You patched me up that night, all right. You took out the bullet but you also inserted a capsule filled with microfilm into my leg and sewed me up, didn't you, Doc? You Commies didn't have to smuggle Complex 90 into Russia—*I did it for you*!"

He was smiling now, a nasty smile, and he started to applaud. The Russians like to applaud—especially for themselves.

I shook the .45 snout at him like a scolding finger. "*That's* why I was taken to that remand prison, Butyrka, not to the K.G.B.'s main facility, the Lubyanka. That's why the warden there was arranging for me to go take my 'physical'—the capsule would have been cut out of me, with me none the wiser, and I'd have been turned over on espionage charges for a nice big show trial."

Giles shrugged. "But you did not cooperate, Mr. Hammer. Instead you cut yourself a path of death and destruction that could never possibly justify one man's desire for survival. How do you sleep at night, Mr. Hammer?"

"I sleep like a baby, pal. Like an innocent babe."

He was shaking his head in disgust. "What now? I suppose you kill me. That's what you do, isn't it? I have given my life to preserving and saving lives, but you, Mr. Hammer, only take and destroy lives. You a monster who holds himself above all others, and the only moral code you follow is an eye for an eye. Vengeance. You are pathetic. Go ahead, Hammer. Kill me. Kill the doctor so instrumental in the achievements of the space program. Kill the scientist whose only goal is maintaining a balance of power in a potentially apocalyptic world. Oh, and be sure to entertain the jury with this amusing tale you've spun."

"No, Doc," I said, shaking my head, "I'm not going to kill you. A guy told me earlier today that there are certain evil sons of a bitches who are more valuable alive than dead, and I think you qualify. You have too much knowledge that Uncle Sam could use—about Russia and K.G.B. espionage, and even Complex 90. It'd be selfish to just bump you the hell off, much as I'd like to."

He glowered at me. He looked a little silly, with his feet dangling like that.

"Okay, Doc," I said. "Hop down off of there like a good boy."

I marched him out into the hall and that was when I heard Lisa Contreaux say, "Thanks for dropping by, Mike," right before she jammed the hypodermic needle in my neck.

CHAPTER TWELVE

I was back in the jungle, huddled in my foxhole, and I could hear the metallic tattoo of machine-gun fire from the Jap nest in the trees. It was cold, dank, but I was sweating, a malaria flare-up maybe. My M-1 was empty and all I had was my .45, and all around me were sprawled the dead and wounded from the last banzai attack, and I was the last whole man and I had to do something. Maybe I'd have a chance if I crawled on my belly through the snarl of brush and around through the trees to come up behind them and empty the .45 into that grinning machine-gunner, but I couldn't make my legs work, and my hand felt rubbery around the Colt's grip, my fingers like sodden sausages, but that goddamn machine-gunning just kept up, as if it were on top of me, and then I wasn't in the foxhole, I was in a tin-roofed, grass-walled hut and the guy from the nest was up there on the roof now, firing down at me, firing right down, and I stared up at the roof watching the bullets dimple the metal, wondering why those slugs didn't tear through that cheap sheet of tin and into me and through me and...

...my eyes opened, and I wasn't in a foxhole or a tin hut.

I was in the backseat of a car with my hands bound behind me, forcing me forward. Felt like tape, adhesive tape. I couldn't see much, and only the bump of the wheels and the groans of the undercarriage on rough road told me I was in a car, a big car, possibly a luxury sedan. I could sense more than see the two big men I was sandwiched between. My head hung and my wits were about me enough to leave it that way, so as not to indicate I was awake, even if a little man inside my brain was beating his bass drum to provide music for the blazing pain behind my eyes.

The rain on the car roof, that machine-gun fire in my fever-dream, was unrelenting. The smell of rain was in the air and on the clothes of those I rode with—a man was at the wheel, a woman next to him, a tall man on my left, a big damn brute on my right. The sky was adding to the bass drum pounding in my brain with its own fireworks show accompanying a banshee orchestra working discordant variations on the climactic passages of "In the Hall of the Mountain King."

Giant cymbals crashed, and the world turned white, and I saw the members of my escort party in a strobe flash.

Dr. Giles was hunkered at the wheel, in a yellow raincoat and floppy matching hat, like a school crossing guard. Eyes straining behind wire-rimmed glasses, he was trying to guide the vehicle through the driving rain, the foggy windshield no help. Lisa Contreaux was in the passenger seat, her Carmen black hair dampened and stringy, her raincoat transparent plastic.

"We'll be fine," the doctor was saying, sounding more confident than he looked. "This road is as straight as it is bumpy. I could drive it in my sleep."

"It feels like that's what you're doing," she said, concerned.

Showing no concern at all were my bookends—a tall skinny cadaver of a man, his cheeks sunken and pockmarked, his eyes hooded and dead behind round black-rimmed glasses. His raincoat was black with water-repellent coating; drops pearled on it. His woolen hat was black and damp, a shorter version of a Cossack cap.

On the other side of me was the bulk of my old friend Comrade Gorlin, a dragon in a tan raincoat. His bald head was egg-shaped, its smoothness disrupted by the Apache cheekbones, his blunt nose with its thick, flaring nostrils, and that bristly brush of a mustache. Droplets of moisture were all over him, as if he were sweating. Maybe he just couldn't be bothered to dry himself off. He had something more important to do.

Being in charge of me.

Where were we? I quickly sensed we were near water, and even over engine thrum and vehicle jostle, I could hear rough, choppy stuff on either side. Harbor sounds found their way through the angry night, like lost children crying for their mothers.

To my left, a beam of light was cutting through the storm, highlighting the driving rain. A boat's beacon? No. Somebody searching for me? No such luck. There was a regularity to the sweep of the beam, though, and a fixed position. *What could it be?*

Then I knew. That was a prison searchlight, nearby but with water between us. Riker's Island? If so, I was beginning to figure out where I was.

"Harmon, don't *hit* it!" Lisa yelped. "It's right in front of us."

Brakes went on, tossing us forward, and it would have been a good time for me to make a move, if my hands weren't bound and my head wasn't exploding.

"Sorry," the doctor said, giving his attractive passenger a sick little smile.

He got a key out of somewhere, and opened the car door, letting the storm come in to momentarily roar at us, as if we were standing too close to a caged beast. Then the man in yellow slicker and droopy matching hat seemed to get swallowed up in all that dark weather until lightning momentarily made the world white again and there he was, not ten feet away, opening a wire gate in a six-foot wire fence topped with barbed wire. Like Butyrka Prison.

After he drove us through, the downpour discouraged the doctor from getting out and locking it behind us. This seemed to raise the ire of Colonel Toy but I couldn't be sure, because Toy spoke in Russian, his voice imperious if nasal.

Giles responded in English—"We'll be fine, Colonel!"—but had obviously understood the man.

Then the car slid under a canopy of overgrown trees and brush right out of my delirium, going down a private drive as rutted as the road that had brought us here. Rain pelted the roof of trees, making the leaves shudder, but when moisture did make it through, it arrived in noisy plops.

Colonel Toy glanced at me, my head still hanging but my slitted eyes taking everything in, and said something else in acid-sounding Russian, a comment again directed at the front seat. This prompted Dr. Giles to glare back at me and say, "Don't bother faking, Mr. Hammer. We know you're awake."

I lifted my head a little, allowed my eyes to open fully. Toy gave me á sneer of a smile—these top Commie bastards were so often every bit as snooty as the blue bloods they despised.

"No witty remarks, Mr. Hammer?" Lisa Contreaux asked,

smiling back over her shoulder like a smug pixie. "Where's that oh-so-tough patter you're noted for?"

I didn't have any for her. Even if I had, I wasn't sure any words could make it past the thick, cottony insides of my mouth.

"Maybe it's the drug," she said, charitably. "Pretty soon it'll wear off and you'll be your sweet old charming self."

What a nasty little piece of business she was.

Yet even with her hair turned by the rain into a nest of wet snakes, she made one lovely damn Medusa.

Finally, the car nosed its way into an overgrown brick courtyard where I could barely make out the looming shapes of buildings in the storm. Then the thunder told the sky to turn on all its electricity, just to give me a better look, and now, for an endless second, I could see the buildings in stark detail.

And I knew right where I was.

This was Sister Island, in the midst of Hell Gate, a particularly hazardous stretch of the East River. Not technically an island, it was connected by a five-mile isthmus near 132nd Street in the Bronx. Its name derived from the Sisters of Mercy who had operated a tuberculosis hospital here in mid-1800s. For a long while the city ran it as a quarantine island, for treatment of smallpox and other deadly infectious diseases—Typhoid Mary herself was sequestered here. Most of the buildings dated to the late nineteenth century, but one modern hospital—Riverview Sanitarium—was constructed during the war as a facility for mentally ill and drug-addicted teenagers. Experimental drugs and shock treatment had been everyday fare around this joint.

Riverview was controversial and notorious for questionable

practices and had been shut down ten years ago. I knew, because I had broken a teenage kid out of this asylum for his mother when her husband had committed the kid, trying to get at some inherited money. The top doc had been bribed by hubby, I discovered. The scandal drove the place under, and I hadn't even had to kill anybody to pull it off.

So returning here, a decade later, had its ironic side, beyond just the notion that a lot of people had said I would wind up in an asylum some day. *Or on some rain-swept, thunder-and-lightning-wracked night.*

Even before the more modern sanitarium had been shut down, most of the older buildings had fallen into disuse and disrepair. The doc guided the car down the overgrown access road that cut between buildings I knew well—a square-ish, gothic-looking pile of bricks that had been a morgue back in quarantine days, and an equally rundown former power plant for the island with its towering smokestack still intact. We rumbled by once magnificent turn-of-the-century structures, now sagging with age and neglect—a maintenance building, which had lost its roof, and the doctors' cottage and a nurses' residence quarters.

The latter gave me a brief warm flash thinking of the cute nurse I'd got next to, when I was plotting that rich kid's escape. I wondered what had become of her.

I wondered what would become of me...

The massive modern building was surprisingly low-slung, only four stories, but its width seemed endless, as if it were a beached steamship, the rounded edges at its widely separated ends like the bow and the stern. At the building's mid-point rose a squat central tower, only one extra story taller, cement steps rising to the main entrance. The tower's gothic look seemed out of place for such an otherwise modernistic structure, X's carved into its face in an Aztec-style design. Maybe that was fitting. Plenty of patients had been sacrificed here to the gods of science.

The rain had dissipated by the time we pulled into the kudzu-choked main parking lot of Riverview Sanitarium. Under a black, grumbling sky, I was hauled by the Dragon from the back of the sedan, which turned out to be a Lincoln—the doc another of these communists who liked nice things. This would have been a good time for me to spring into action and turn the tables on my captors, only my legs were rubbery and my fingers were numb, perhaps from the tightness of the adhesive tape binding my wrists together.

Adhesive tape did make sense as impromptu handcuffs—they had not been expecting me to show up at the doc's private practice. They'd had to make do. Giles had said he had run late because of walk-in patients—likely among them, Comrade Gorlin, who had after all been put through the mill in the brawl and shoot-out in my apartment.

Gorlin practically dragged me up the many cement steps to the entrance into the central tower. The trouble I gave him wasn't that of a rebel but of a sack of sand—I was still woozy and half-dazed from whatever Lisa Contreaux had dosed me with. She sure hadn't had a gentle touch. My neck ached and burned as if a boil were coming to a head.

The big doors weren't locked, and Giles held one open like a genial doorman as the Dragon dragged me inside and across a lobby empty of furnishings but long on peeling green paint. The scratching of fleeing rats, hearing human entry, was the only indication of activity within these walls. Where the elevators had been, doors were gone, cars absent, revealing empty space where wires and cables dangled.

In ten years, the place had got seriously run down, but it still looked vaguely habitable, like a slum building that just needed a less venal landlord. The doctor and Lisa, their raincoats still leaving a damp trail, went on ahead of us up a stairwell. Gorlin dragged me five endless flights, Colonel Toy bringing up the rear, and it wore the hell out of me.

But it wasn't all bad.

Because I was starting to feel something in my hands, and my legs were under me now, working damn near the way legs should, and the little guy inside my head had traded in his bass drum for a kid's toy snare, doing little irritating rolls that were still a hell of a lot better than *boom boom boom*. On the third landing, I was able to pause and catch my breath because Dr. Giles was stopping to catch his. The pain in my neck was worse now than the one behind my eyes.

Progress.

Every floor we glimpsed was dirty and flung with refuse and dotted with rat shit, often with fallen ceiling tiles that looked half-eaten. There was less peeling paint because the walls were yellow ceramic tile with just an upper edging of plaster. Still, the place was a mess. That this had been a hospital once made the filth seem somehow filthier.

When we got to the fifth floor of the truncated tower, some

sweeping up had been done, clearing a path. Otherwise we were met by more mess. Then we followed Dr. Giles as he pushed through double doors into another world.

A light switch was thrown and florescent overheads revealed a good-size science laboratory. Spotless. Pristine. Goddamn gleaming. While no repainting had been done on the edging of plaster wall above the ceramic tile, it had been scraped and any residue swept away. This could have been a top lab in any hospital or research facility. The counters and benches had the expected beakers and burners and test tubes and meters and microscopes, but also sophisticated equipment I could never hope to identify.

Obviously, much of Giles' research had been conducted here, not at Manheim University. *Some* work had been done at the school, perhaps even the Complex 90 breakthrough itself achieved, but the final stages had been performed here, in secret, with Soviet funding.

I just slumped there with Gorlin propping me up—and now I *was* faking, because I could have stood on my own two feet, but why not let the son of a bitch wear himself out? We had paused because Dr. Giles and Lisa Contreaux were hanging up their wet raincoats in a closet. Giles still wore his white smock and Lisa was in another of her silk blouse and pencil skirt combos, this one pink and red. Showing her true colors at last.

She was reaching for a white smock from an adjacent closet when she asked, "Shall I prepare the dosage, Harmon?"

Harmon, she called him—not "doctor" or "Dr. Giles," or even "Giles." Harmon. The familiarity was telling.

"Yes, please do—thank you, dear."

Well, that was telling, too.

"I can manage Mr. Hammer quite easily," Giles told her. "That drug won't wear off entirely for several hours. He's going to be as easy to handle as a lamb."

They didn't know much about me, or my constitution, did they? The doc should have stuck to curing the outer space flu.

Colonel Toy was standing off to one side looking quietly pissed off. He said, "You should have locked that gate."

English now.

"We'll be fine," the doctor said, amiable but with just the tiniest edge of irritation.

Toy reached inside his black raincoat and withdrew a Makarov pistol. The doc flinched, and Lisa frowned, but if they thought they were about to be threatened, they had read their comrade wrong.

"I will go down and guard the gate," the cadaverous figure in the abbreviated Cossack cap said rather grandly. "*We* do things right."

Meaning the K.G.B., of course.

In a curt manner that suggested he was giving orders, Toy spoke to the Dragon in Russian, then said to the doctor, "Comrade Gorlin will be on guard below. In the lobby."

Giles said, "Before he goes, the comrade needs to lend me a hand here. Just to get Mr. Hammer situated."

Toy seemed annoyed, but nodded curtly.

Then Gorlin hauled me through a push door into an adjoining room, a smaller one that opened off the lab. The doc reached in and flipped a switch on more fluorescence.

This area had been given a cursory cleaning but was not in the sanitary condition of its neighbor, and seemed strictly for storage. Counters rimmed the room, stacked with cardboard boxes of medical and scientific supplies. It may have once been an examining room or perhaps a modest operating room. The big object in its midst seemed to confirm the latter.

An antique operating table, a baroque-looking affair with a metal base painted white but chipped away here and there, stood dead center. A big metal wheel allowed for adjustments to the three-piece table, whose trio of steel surfaces had been cleaned and perhaps even polished, though they stopped short of gleaming, more a flat, dull glow. Odd, serrated loops of steel near where a patient's arms and feet would rest appeared to be ports for restraints.

Giles read my confusion and he beamed at me, as benign as a country doctor circa 1920—the major difference was the eyes behind those wire-framed glasses. They were a little crazy.

"No, Mr. Hammer, I'm not performing experimental operations using equipment out of the dark ages. When we scouted this property for our possible use—and we are renting it *quite* legally, you will I'm sure be relieved to know—I spotted this little beauty. A very valuable antique, dating back to quarantine days. I had it moved in here for now. Eventually I'll have it moved out, and into my personal collection… Uh, Comrade Gorlin?"

Giles gestured toward the operating table, indicating the doctor's wish that I be deposited on that three-tiered steel bed. The Dragon picked me up like I was his unlucky bride and, in lieu of a threshold to cross, slammed me down there. On my back, my bound hands still behind me.

It hurt like hell, getting rudely dumped like that. But I was glad to be feeling pain somewhere besides my neck or inside my head, glad especially to have the numbness leave my fingers so that I could move and wiggle them again. Yes my wrists were bound together, but now at least I had some motion in my hands. Just in case I wanted to play patty-cake with myself...

...or maybe wanted to work on getting that safety razor blade from the slit in my belt, and use it to cut into and through these adhesive-tape bonds. So much easier than dealing with rope. Still, I had to turn and twist my wrists without giving away what I was up to. I did this as carefully, as subtly as I could...

In her white smock, Lisa pushed in through the door, and she had another hypo in her hand. Definitely a one-note kind of nurse.

"Shall I administer it, Doctor?"

Not "Harmon," now—but then things were getting serious, right? They were about to perform an operation.

"I handle that, thanks," Giles said, taking the hypo from her. "Get his pants off him, would you?"

"Yes, Doctor."

She came over and smiled at me as she started to undo my belt.

Damn! I almost had that blade out! If she yanked my damn trousers off, taking my belt along for the ride, I could say goodbye to any hope of escape...

I grinned gamely at her. "And to think I was looking forward to this moment."

Her smile seemed genuinely amused if a little confused. "Were you, really? *This* moment?"

"Sure," I said. "The moment when you peeled my pants off of me, and we got down to business."

"Ah," she said, and shook her head. Some moisture from the still damp mass of gypsy curls flicked at me. "I *thought* we might hear from that rough wit of yours."

"Anything to please you, baby."

"Bravado, Mike? In the face of death? I don't know whether to admire you or pity you."

"Can't it be both?"

I had almost had the thing!

Her fingers were undoing my belt buckle. "You have such an astonishingly high opinion of yourself, Mike. You *really* thought I desired *you?* That all my talk of scientific and intellectual pursuits was just so much blather? That what I needed, what I *wanted*, was a man with wide shoulders, a two-fisted he-man who packed a big... *gun...?*"

She unzipped my pants.

"You were right, of course, about Dennis Dorfman," she admitted. "Poor Dennis, very smart boy, if not quite brilliant. But he *was* close to the head of the space research project at Manheim, and it was handy being able to manipulate him for what I needed... for what *Harmon* needed... and such child's play to keep track of what Dennis knew about what we were up to. So that if he ever discovered or even just guessed what strides Harmon was actually making, we could do something about it."

"So this kid you were sleeping with became just another casualty for the greater good, huh? Like Ralph Marley. Or a young Russian girl named Zora. And an American G.I. called Des Casey."

"Like Marley, yes. The other two are names I'm afraid I've never heard before. Do you know the names of the forty-five people *you* killed, Mike?"

"You knew Dennis's name."

"I did."

"Did you run him down yourself, Lisa?"

"Does that matter? No, I didn't. I hired it done. That's the thing about so many Americans, Mike. They'll do anything for money."

She yanked my pants down around my ankles, the steel of the table cold against my bare legs.

But the steel of that little razor blade felt warm between my fingers.

The scar and redness in my thigh where that bullet had caught me seemed to stand out under the bright light.

"No, Mike, I am not in the least attracted to big, strong, brutal idiots like you. To me, a *real* man is Dr. Harmon Giles. A man who cares about science. And about world peace."

"And I'm sure an old bird like the doc," I said, as my fingers worked the blade into the adhesive tape, "is drawn to you strictly for that brain of yours. Just a bonus that it's stuck inside a stacked young body."

Her dark eyes jumped with anger. "You are a stupid son of a bitch, Mike Hammer."

"Like I haven't heard that before."

The doctor had been working at the counter. Now he turned toward me, with the hypo in one hand and with the other raised in a palm-out, calming fashion. "Step back outside, Nurse. I won't be needing any further assistance."

This time he called her "nurse." Just to make her feel official and not merely his young honey. The doc had brains, all right. Lisa was right about that much.

She slipped out.

He was hovering over me with the hypo.

"What's that, Doc? A sedative?"

An amused smile curved under his mustache. "Of a sort. You see, Mr. Hammer, transporting you back to Russia is out of the question now. You have been successful in disrupting our plans, and you may take satisfaction in that."

"You bet your ass."

"But it is still necessary to retrieve that capsule with the Complex 90 formula. It was never intended to be inside of you for quite so long, which is why you've suffered some discomfort."

"And now you'll relieve my discomfort, Doc?"

"In a way. We wouldn't want that capsule turning up in an autopsy, as you yourself noted, should your body wash up to shore. No, not a sedative, Mr. Hammer. You see, in the case of *this* surgery, it's not required for you to be alive at the outset."

He leaned in and my right arm came out from under me and my hand moved around to clutch his wrist and my other hand came around to grab onto his smock and hold him there as, in one swift motion, I jammed the needle into his neck and my thumb pressed down on his, sending whatever poison he'd intended for me into his jugular.

He back-pedaled from his antique operating table, arms windmilling, hypo still stuck in his neck, and he knocked into the counter and slid to the floor and sat there in astonishment.

Lisa rushed in and began screaming.

He looked past me at her.

He said in a very small voice, "Help. Help me. Darling... help..."

She rushed to him, knelt to him as if at an altar. Her hand reached for the hypo jutting from his neck, but hesitated. "What can I *do*, Harmon? What can I do?"

"Ah, let him heal himself," I said.

I had slipped off the table and was about to pull my trousers back on, out of a sense of decorum if nothing else, when she whirled to her feet and where she got the little gun from, I have no idea. It was just a little revolver, a .22, a purse gun, and it was no real problem. Not unless she shot me in the head, like in the right eye for instance. Where she was pointing it.

There wasn't much space between us—all three of us were on the same side of the baroque table, her and me and the doc. All I'd have to do was jump her to put an end to this.

But she had caught me with my pants down. Literally down around my ankles, and I would trip over myself if I made a move.

"That's right, Mike. Look down that barrel. Look into that little round hole filled with the darkness that will swallow you up." Her voice was shaking but her hand was steady. "*Look what you've done!*"

She herself didn't look, but I did as asked: Dr. Harmon Giles was sitting there with a needle in his neck and his eyes as wide as they were unseeing, spittle and vomit decorating his slack open mouth, his complexion already as pale as the white base of the antique operating table.

"A man like *you!*" Her eyes were wild. "Uncouth, unschooled, a mental midget with his brains in his *fists!* For the world to lose a man like… like *Harmon*… a man of such brilliance, to a neanderthal like *you*. This was a *man*, a great man, who only wanted to better the world. I can't *allow* it, Mike. I can't allow a creature like you to exist. Your existence, Mike, in the absence of Harmon's presence, is an insult. An insult to science. To peace. To the betterment of—"

A whip crack stopped her mid-sentence.

Only it wasn't the crack of a whip, not really, rather the sound of a .32 Browning as a spray of the brains Lisa Contreaux was so proud of flew out the hole in the side of her head to splatter on the wall like so much more waste matter in this pesthole husk of a hospital.

"She talked too much," Velda said, at the door, the nose of her .32 curling smoke. In a black raincoat, her hair matted down and damp, my beautiful partner had never looked better.

"I was beginning to get worried," I said.

"You think *that* character…" She gestured with the gun to the slumped, dead Giles. "…could shake *my* tail? Get your pants on. I knew you couldn't keep 'em on around that little bitch."

We stepped into the lab side by side and I said, "What about the other two?"

"I dealt with that tall skull-faced character at the gate. I didn't kill him, since we need a live specimen. He's bleeding from the shoulder, and ruining the inside of the trunk of that heap of yours. Can't be helped."

"What about the Dragon?"

"Is *that* who he is? I just saw a big guy in a raincoat milling around the lobby through a rain-smeared window. I came in the back way, up the rear stairs."

"Well," I said, my shoulders tightening, "if Gorlin heard that shot, he's on his way up here now…"

She was handing me my spare .45, which she'd carried in a raincoat pocket. "He may not have heard it. We're a bunch of floors up from him. Let's go back down the rear stairs."

"I want him. This time I *want* him."

She put a hand on my shoulder and showed me a patient face. "Let me take you down the back stairs, and then you can come around and—"

That was when the Dragon burst into the lab.

Comrade Gorlin had his Makarov out, and he raised it at me, his thick-mustached lip curling back to expose those massive yellow teeth in a snarl, his brow furrowed but his eyes wide, but before either he or I could fire, Velda was blasting with the Browning, screaming at him and just blasting away, and she unloaded the thing at him, tearing holes in him and his tan raincoat, catching him in the shoulder and arm of the hand holding the Makarov, the weapon dropping from useless fingers, another slug nicking him in the left leg, before he stumbled back through those doors and out.

Velda had hurt him, no question, but her firing had been atypically erratic, and I looked over at her and she was panting like she'd run a marathon, her eyes and nostrils flared, her mouth open in a silent scream, the cords in her neck taut, standing out in bas relief.

"What?" I said.

"*That's* him? That's your Dragon?"

"Yeah! Of course."

She gripped my sleeve. "Your *Dragon*, Mike... he's *my* torturer. *That's him!* That's the K.G.B. torturer who—"

But she never finished—I was already in pursuit. I could hear him on the stairs, as he tried to run but his shot-up arm and especially the nicked leg were slowing him, staggering him. I took those stairs three at a time, risking the refuse and clutter that could have tripped me up, just racing down with no regard to the risk, and on the third-floor landing I caught up with him, only I didn't shoot him, I tossed the .45 aside and I threw myself at him and on him and brought him down hard. He was wounded, all right, but a wounded beast is the most dangerous kind, and with his good hand he punched and flailed, and both knees worked at my midsection and groin. We rolled in the filth, the paint peelings, the brick dust, the rat dung, and it covered us in an awful gray, as his one big fist hammered at me but my two big fists smashed into him and smashed into him and smashed into him, and whenever a blow caught his wounded shoulder, he howled in rage and pain, until finally he grew sluggish and his hand fell limp. When I crawled off him, breathing hard, wiping blood off my face with a dirty paw, he lay on his back on the filthy floor, breathing hard too, but irregularly, hurt inside, things broken, tissue damaged, organs bleeding, though he was not dying, not yet. He was not even unconscious.

I felt her nearness before I saw her.

Velda was standing on the stairs where she had watched much of it, the Browning still in her grasp.

"Give me a hand with him," I said.

"What?"

"Just do it."

We hauled him up the stairs, much as he had hauled me earlier. He helped a little, figuring I was getting him somewhere out of this grime. As a prisoner of war, he expected ethical and humane treatment. But this was a cold war and my response would be in kind.

Then we were walking him through the lab and into the little room where the dead doctor and nurse waited. I wouldn't be needing their assistance.

I slammed him up onto the operating table like a great big fish I'd landed onto a boat deck. I could hear him breathing, moaning, whimpering. A dragon whimpering. Wasn't *that* goddamn undignified…

"Honey," I said, and I held my hand near her face, but didn't touch her, not with all that bloody muck on me. "You go find a phone. Call Rickerby. And then call Pat. But there's no hurry."

She looked at me confused. "No hurry?"

"No." I went over to the counter where Giles had been preparing my surgery and found the scalpel.

"This is going to take a while," I said.

ABOUT THE AUTHORS

MICKEY SPILLANE and **MAX ALLAN COLLINS** collaborated on numerous projects, including twelve anthologies, three films and the *Mike Danger* comic book series.

SPILLANE was the bestselling American mystery writer of the twentieth century. He introduced Mike Hammer in *I, the Jury* (1947), which sold in the millions, as did the six tough mysteries that soon followed. The controversial P.I. has been the subject of a radio show, comic strip, and several television series; numerous gritty movies have been made from Spillane novels, notably director Robert Aldrich's seminal film *noir, Kiss Me Deadly* (1955), and *The Girl Hunters* (1963), in which the writer played his famous hero.

COLLINS has earned an unprecedented nineteen Private Eye Writers of America "Shamus" nominations, winning for *True Detective* (1983) and *Stolen Away* (1993) in his Nathan Heller series, which includes the recent *Target Lancer*. His graphic novel *Road to Perdition* is the basis of the Academy Award-winning film. A filmmaker in the Midwest, he has had half a dozen feature screenplays produced, including *The Last Lullaby* (2008), based on his innovative Quarry series. As "Barbara Allan," he and his wife Barbara write the "Trash 'n' Treasures" mystery series (recently *Antiques Chop*).

Both Spillane (who died in 2006) and Collins received the Private Eye Writers of America life achievement award, the Eye.

AVAILABLE FROM TITAN BOOKS

THE MATT HELM SERIES

DONALD HAMILTON

The long-awaited return of the United States' toughest
special agent.

Death of a Citizen
The Wrecking Crew
The Removers
The Silencers (June 2013)
Murderers' Row (August 2013)
The Ambushers (October 2013)
The Shadowers (December 2013)
The Ravagers (February 2014)

TITANBOOKS.COM

PRAISE FOR DONALD HAMILTON

"Donald Hamilton has brought to the spy novel the authentic hard realism of Dashiell Hammett; and his stories are as compelling, and probably as close to the sordid truth of espionage, as any now being told."
Anthony Boucher, *The New York Times*

"This series by Donald Hamilton is the top-ranking American secret agent fare, with its intelligent protagonist and an author who consistently writes in high style. Good writing, slick plotting and stimulating characters, all tartly flavored with wit."
Book Week

"Matt Helm is as credible a man of violence as has ever figured in the fiction of intrigue."
The New York Sunday Times

"Fast, tightly written, brutal, and very good..."
Milwaukee Journal

TITANBOOKS.COM

PRAISE FOR HELEN MACINNES

"The queen of spy writers." *Sunday Express*

"Definitely in the top class." *Daily Mail*

"The hallmarks of a MacInnes novel of suspense are as individual and as clearly stamped as a Hitchcock thriller." *The New York Times*

"She can hang her cloak and dagger right up there with Eric Ambler and Graham Greene." *Newsweek*

"More class than most adventure writers accumulate in a lifetime." *Chicago Daily News*

"A sophisticated thriller. The story builds up to an exciting climax." *Times Literary Supplement*

"An atmosphere that is ready to explode with tension... a wonderfully readable book." *The New Yorker*

TITANBOOKS.COM